The Adventures
of
Mother and Jasper

The Adventures

of

Mother and Jasper

Patrice Kilham

Hamhill Press

2014

Hamhill Press

hamhillpress@gmail.com

ISBN: 069224512x

ISBN-13:978-0692245125

Printed in the United States of America

Dedicated to Bob,

who helped make Jasper real.

and

To Mom and Dad, who have always been,

and will always be, in my heart.

Note from the Author

While many of the situations that Mother and Jasper have faced during their ongoing adventures may seem very familiar to the residents of a few New Hampshire towns, they are in fact, completely a creation of the writer. All the characters are fictional, though their traits may be not so difficult to find around a small town.

My husband, Bob, and I created the characters of Jasper and Mother during a drive down the road to retrieve a free pick-up cap from a neighboring yard. The cap was a tad long for my husband's S-10, but never being people who turn down "free," we plunked it up there, tied it on with some rope and duct tape and toted it on home, each of us with an arm out the window holding it down.

We thought it was pretty special to have found such a nice little truck cap, absolutely free. There was a set of louvered windows on each side, complete with screening *and* the inside was finished with genuine wood grain-like paneling. Now the truck was a camp-*ah* (camper ... for those who don't yet understand "Jasper-eze.")

We imagined the adventures that could now happen with this beautiful camper, which evolved, and eventually, devolved into laughter and silliness. Somehow that free truck cap gave birth to Jasper and Mother. Seeing life though their eyes over the years has helped me to gain a different perspective on the sometimes annoying, but always humorous predicaments of small town living.

I hope you enjoy reading these stories as much as I enjoyed creating them.

Author's Disclaimer

Any resemblance of characters, names or incidents to any I have known, or anyplace that I may have lived is purely coincidental. All stories are fictional and, though may be loosely based on the author's personal experiences in a small town, none are *completely* true.

Adventures

Cast of "Charactahs"

Jasper

Mother

Chuckie Elvis Stockdale- Mother's nephew

Martha Stockdale- Mother's sister

Cal Deckland-Jasper's best buddy from high school, road agent
and waste facility manager

Ed Peterson- Chief of police

Doc Nickles-town physician

Inoculina Nickles- Doc's daughter

Marion- Doc's nurse

Tetra Hedron- town clerk

Polly Hedron- sister of above

Noreen- works at Village Store

Kelly- Noreen's husband

Bethy Deckland- Cal's wife

Recycle- Cal's dog

Jake Deckland- Cal's brother,

Joe Vespucci Jr- marina owner & ski craft salesman

Gertie and Don- Mother's good friend' on the Lake

George and Melinda Hubbard- friends by the school soccer field

Dr. Jerimiah Calef -town doc

Ellie Mercer- Librarian

Miriam Standish- Dr. Calef's nurse

Old Man Gawmer- local farmer -pigs, pumpkins

Officer Tony Seneli- Part time town police officer

Cynthia Gordon -Village Elementary School vice principal

Miss Feinhaus- Chuckie's teacher

George Edwards- 87 year old resident

The Dog Lady

Nacky Sweinworth- President of the Coalition of Free Thinkers

Joe Garner- town resident

Seth Makey- resident and skunk thrower

Emma vanShuke- Member of the Ladies Guild

Father McDonald- Pastor of the Church of the Holy Rosary

Rob Roundtree- Bruncheon bacon hog

The Dog

The Adventures
of
Mother and Jasper

Mother's Dream Boat

The winter winds were howling and the lake was a frozen wasteland. Despite the nasty weather, Jasper had dragged Mother along to the annual boat show down to the Armory. For Jasper, the show was a wonderland of summer fantasies. The drab green and cement interior gave way to the glistening sides of bass boats, powerboats, sailboats, sailboards and kayaks. The trip was an excuse to talk fishing with anyone Jasper could get to listen. Mother, having heard all of the stories, truth and lies, wandered off in search of a cup of coffee and maybe a hot dog with mustard and a touch of relish.

Sipping her way down the long aisles full of fiberglass and foam, she paused to dawb at a bit of mustard from her lip. That was when her head was

1

turned and she wandered into a booth draped in shimmering turquoise curtains and a wide screen TV. There, a video of sparkling water caught Mother's eye. Across the water zoomed a nymph, a most lovely woman, atop the "modern stallion- the personal water craft," or so the man on the video said.

Mesmerized, she watched the machine hop about on the water, and sure enough, if that vixen of a girl didn't start looking an awful lot like herself in her precocious pre-Jasper years. A tail of shiny dark hair flitted behind her and her skin was tan and glowing in the sun. *That* girl was looking toward a future that had *every* possibility.

"May I help you, Miss?" Mother startled, blushed and finally noticed the trickle of coffee that was spilling onto the floor of the armory from her cup.

"Ohh..I'm sorry, uhh..,"she stammered, looking up at a gorgeous, golden skinned young man in a sports coat and jeans. Self consciously, she glanced over her shoulder. Then Mother bravely announced, "Ayuh! *You* surely *can* help me."

When the delivery truck arrived several months later, Jasper was as wary as a junkyard dog. The Vespucci Marina truck backed slowly up the driveway on that sunny afternoon in June. Jasper hurried his way over from his workshop, stumbling over the Dog on the way out of the door. Mother was just stood in the dooryard with a satisfied yet dreamy look on her face.

"FELLA! HEY! You there!" hollered Jasper. "Hey, what you doin' here? You gotta have the wrong address here." Two young men hopped out of the vehicle and began to unload a brand new silver and pink personal water craft, with trailer and a bright pink personal flotation vest (Coast Guard approved, of course.) Mother flung open the kitchen door and skipped across the lawn. She snatched the clipboard from young Joe Vespucci Jr. He grinned the same glistening smile, which she had noticed when she bought the craft with her hard-earned coupon cash.

Jasper stood in the middle of the yard, mouth hanging wide with nothing productive to add except a loud and plaintive "But, *Mothuh*?"

Joe Jr. eased the craft up beside Jasper's old truck and propped it up securely. He swung back to the truck, tipping his hat to Mother.

"Enjoy it now! Be sure to call me to let me know how you like your little machine!" He slipped his business card along with the receipt into Mother's hand with a little squeeze. She eyed the boat dreamily, as if a knight in shining armor had just arrived to save her from her distress.

"*But, Mothuh!*" sputtered Jasper."What is going on here? Where did this thing come from?"

Mother, feeling a might spritely, danced over to Jasper, catching him in her arms and waltzed over the lawn.

"Isn't it just beautiful Jasper? It came from Vespucci's Marina. Isn't he a lovely young man? Now I gotta get it down to Gertie and Don's dock on the lake to-morrow. I better go study up on these directions!"

With that, she toddled off, leaving Jasper in the yard, completely flabbergasted.

The morning dawned gloriously sunny, and by 7 o'clock, Mother was off, having commandeered Jasper's truck. Jasper had lurched out of bed when he heard the engine crank with it's usual BRAAAAAAT but he was only able to get a glimpse of Mother's trail of dust.

"My truck? What the...? Aw, *Mothuh*!"He struggled into a pair of overalls and took off in hot pursuit in his wife's shopping car, an equally ancient but always tidy Toyota. *"Gawd, dam, it!"*

He finally caught up with her at the town boat launch, just as she was about to submerge most of his truck in the lake.

"*Jay*-sus, woman!" He cried through the open window, peeling into the boat launch with a spray of dirt. "Mothuh, have you *completely* lost your mind?"

Mother was completely focused on the task at hand, so took no notice of the raging man who shrieked at her from the window of a vaguely familiar auto. She was solely focused on the adventure that loomed ahead. On the ski craft, the wind would blow through her hair and she would glide upon the water like that nymph! Joe Vespucci had described it to her and she believed him. She would be reborn. She would be young again.

The trailer eased into the water smoothly, which surprised both Jasper and Mother. She had never actually unloaded a boat before. She had watched Jasper do it hundreds of times and had picked up more than they both realized.

She leaped from the cab, tossing the keys to Jasper as he sputtered over to the vehicle. Mother peeled off her housecoat to reveal her conservative swimming dress. She donned her pink life jacket. Wisely she had purchased the complete package from the Vespucci's including a silver helmet with a glare proof visor, which she now snapped into place, as she waded up to the winch and released the ski craft into the water. Before Jasper could spit out any further protest she was up in the seat and had the key in the ignition.

"But Mother, don't you think you should wait a minute now...." Jasper's advice was drowned out by the revving of the engine. She was off and away, a displaced lock of gray hair blew from beneath the helmet and a pair of substantial thighs clenched tightly on each side of the saddle. Mother accelerated loudly and quickly turned the corner around First Island.

Jasper did the only thing he could, under the circumstances. He adjourned to the Village store for coffee. Mother had left the house in such a tizzy she had not even fixed him any breakfast.

Being that they lived in a small town, the word was already out that Mother was out on her very own personal watercraft and that Jasper had no idea how it had come to be. He just garumped unintelligibly at anyone who asked about the new acquisition and made excuses to leave early.

He decided to wander up to Gertie and Don's to see if Mother had landed. He pulled in the yard and could see the circular wake of the ski-thing doing donuts in the lake behind the tidy home. Slamming the car door sternly, Jasper hustled his way out to the dock where Don and Gertie stood, laughing at Mother's antics.

"Well, Jasper, what do you think about our own Esther Williams of the ski craft set? Isn't it terrific? I know she's been waiting on this day all spring! I never thought the thing would be so much fun." Gertie nudged her husband and suggested with a wink, "What do you think, Donny? Maybe I ought to get *myself* one of those from that cutie Joe Vespucci Jr.!"

At this point, Mother turned in towards the dock. With a swoosh, she slid the ski craft onto shore and hopped off like a woman of twenty-five. Her cheeks glowed pink and now a ring of gray sun-kissed curls peeked from beneath her silver helmet.

"Mothuh? Mothuh, I demand an explanation now!" spit Jasper as he stamped his foot and looked as if he was going to cry.

"Don & I will get some fresh coffee going. How about you get this settled now and come on up to the house in a few minutes after you chat a bit... and join us for a cup?" Gertie pulled Don and they quickly exited the scene.

"Now Jasp-ah don't you say anything! I don't care what you think! I *am* keepin' it." Mother unclasped the chinstrap on her helmet, and removed it from her head. She carefully hung it on the handle of the machine and returned a hardened gaze toward Jasper. Arms crossed defiantly across her chest, she rallied on. "I like it Jasper. It's mine and I *am* keepin' it."

"Now Mothuh! This is just ridiculous! You hardly even go swimmin' any more!" Jasper reasoned. "And what in Gawd's name are your church lady-friends gonna say when they hear about this? Ain't you gonna be embarrassed?"

Mother's defiant posture wilted noticeably and the sparkle in her eyes dimmed. Jasper had only meant to talk some sense into her. He had never meant make her sad. His head of steam vanished like a wisp of a cloud in a northeaster.

"Aww, Mothuh," Jasper cajoled. "Come on now. Don't you start sniveling" He ran his rough, hard worn fingertips along her cheek. She looked up at him contritely.

"Now Jasp-ah, I *really* meant to tell you, but somehow the time never seemed right. That little machine just seems to be built for me! Somehow I just knew I had to have it. Don't you think I look pretty good on it?" Mother peered up at him through the tips of her lashes and fished for his favor.

"Well, of course you do, Mothuh. You still look like the fine little water lily I knew when I married you." Jasper replied without hesitation. No matter how crazy Mother seemed to him sometimes, she was still his gal. "Now let's go get some coffee and you can tell me all about it! Next time you leave my truck out of your plans. I thought it was going under for a bit there!"

Having regained his control, Jasper strode off toward the house, and Mother just smiled with one sidelong glance at the silver and pink craft that, for today, would keep all her dreams of afloat.

The Dog

Jasper lapped his fingers liberally and reached up to paste back a few stray hairs with spit.

"There." he stated with satisfaction as he studied himself in the hall mirror. "I'm ready."

"Where are you off to Jasper?" Mother asked him, looking up from the pan of apples she was peeling. She winked at him, "You're fixed awful fine for coffee at the store. Do you have a girlfriend that I haven't heard about?"

"Not exactly, Mothuh." Jasper went on seriously. Jasper wasn't above flirting but Mothuh knew that no woman with even one brain cell would ever have him. "I am goin' down to Town Hall to register the Dog this morning."

"OH…. Lordy!" sighed Mother quietly. "Gawd help us all!"

Jasper's dog was one of the oddest-looking animals. Its back and shoulders were covered with wild, wiry curls. Its rump hair was so short and smooth it appeared as if it had been worn bald. The Dog had huge pointy ears that stuck straight up off its minuscule dachshund-sized head. It's snakey, whip of a tail wagged incessantly, reeking havoc wherever he went. But, Jasper's dog was a happy dog.

The Dog had actually adopted Jasper. Cal Deckland was road agent but because the town was so small he also had charge of the local dump. Early one Saturday morning, Cal had opened up the incinerator building and the Dog was there. The tiny weird fuzz ball was sitting amidst a huge pile of trash, wagging his tail furiously; the tail whipped the trash into a hurricane of dust and grime, but Cal swore the Dog had actually smiled at him.

Cal Deckland loved dogs. He had already rescued three, all from the dump. He had even named one Recycle and won a contest on a radio show for most original pet name. However, his wife wasn't about to let him bring another animal into their house.

Jasper had been dogless since his old beagle ate one too many of Mother's shoes many years before. It had choked on the sensible heel. This strange little pup was so pitiful, Jasper could hardly say no when Cal showed up at the store with it. The Dog had crawled up into the cab of Jasper's rusty, old truck, dragging its long rope of a tail behind him. They had come out after coffee to find The Dog in the driver's seat, holding a half chewed book of road maps in his mouth. The seat beside him was striped with mud, sand and other unidentifiable muck. The remnants of the seat belt shoulder harness hung in shreds from the doorframe.

"Welp, guess he's made himself at home, Cal. I better go back in for some cans of Calo and some kibble, eh?"

Cal was happy.
Cal's wife was happy.
Jasper was happy.
The Dog was happy

Mother was *not*.

When Jasper brought The Dog home that day, it bounded into the kitchen joyfully, its tail wiping clear every surface it came near. Mother promptly escorted it, and Jasper, not so joyfully, back onto the porch.

"Jaspah? What in heaven's name is *that*? And what ever behooved you to invite it into *my* kitchen?" Despite herself, Mother reached down to scratch The

Dog just behind one of his huge pointed ears. "Well it is..... er, unique! Look at him- is he smiling? ... But that tail is a terror!" The more she scratched, the faster the tail whipped, taking down several potted plants, two citronella candles, a seat cushion and a pan of potpourri, which scattered across the wood floor, crunching beneath their feet.

"So, can he stay, Mothuh? Puh-lease, hun?" Jasper gazed at her with his own puppy dog eyes. "I'll take care of it, I promise, Mothuh."

Against her better instincts she gave in and The Dog became a part of their family.

Jasper found that dog ownership had several stages of responsibility. His first assignment was to take The Dog to the vet. Jasper set no store in doctors for himself and did not necessarily agree that his dog needed such special care. The animal ate and processed almost any substance without hesitation- cushions, sticks and twigs, written material, Brillo pads, and any number of absolutely unidentifiable outcomes. Mother had convinced him that The Dog needed to get his shots and be checked for parasites by Doc Nickles down to the Veterinary.

Doc had inspected, injected, de-wormed and decontaminated The Dog. The Dog sat on the shiny metal table, grinning and wagging his whip of a tail. Doc had called in his daughter, and vet tech, Inoculina, just to restrain The Dog's tail during the exam.

"So what's his name?" asked Doc Nickles, his pen poised over a form verifying the current rabies vaccination. Doc had a particular affection for word play and creative names.

Jasper stared at the Dog for a moment and replied thoughtfully.

"Well, jeez Doc, I haven't thought one up yet. I figgered he'd just tell me. I've just been callin' him The Dog, so I suppose that's his name now."

"Jasper, are you sure? Don't you want to name him Bingo or Rex or something more of, well, an actual *name*? I think you might run into some trouble down to Town Hall. You know how feisty Polly gets down there about her paperwork." Doc laid the pad and his pen down on the table. The Dog nipped it into position and settled down for a satisfying chew while the men were distracted.

"Nay-uh! He's The Dog. I can't be making him have a name he doesn't own." Jasper squatted down to look The Dog in the eye, wrestling the spitty nub of a pen from its mouth and handed it to the vet. "Here you are, Doc. Look him in the eyes and tell me that's not his name now?"

Doc had known Jasper long enough to know that arguing was futile. He scratched at the pad binding with the half pen, which remarkably still wrote, though Doc wondered what percentage was ink versus saliva.

"Well, here's all your paperwork Jasper and The Dog's rabies tag. Don't forget it's got to be *on* the dog, not your rearview mirror this time, okay? Good luck getting this one by Polly! You are gonna need it, Jasper!"

"Just bill me, Doc! And that woman will just have to deal with it." Jasper grabbed The Dog's leash and headed for the door. He crumpled the certificate into his shirt pocket. "Thanks Doc!"

The Dog adapted to the household easily, though Mother found it proactive to remove all knickknacks, remote controls, magazines, well, everything not stapled down, to higher elevations to avoid The Dog's table-clearing tail.

Now, Jasper had intended to register The Dog the day after they had been to the vet, but somehow time had gotten away from him and now months had passed. Being as he had coffee with the police chief every morning, it was the chief's habit to give The Dog a biscuit on his way out to the cruiser everyday. Jasper didn't see why he had to fill out some stupid papers. He just hated to go down to that infernal office at Town Hall. Every time he went in to do some business, he always seemed to need something else. Those women there were never happy with just filling in the paper, taking his money, and letting him leave. No. For his car he needed to verify some number that was smudged. Ed had to come over and find his VIN embossed on the truck! Then he had to pay his property taxes twice a year, which was just an exercise in elevating his blood pressure as far as he was concerned.

Early in May, a postcard arrived, advising them that the "Town Offices have been made aware that there was an unregistered male canine in residence at this address" and would they please come down and register him now.

Mother reminded him that The Dog was still unofficial and, technically, illegal! And how would that look for Ed, the chief of police to be feeding biscuits to an illegal animal every day?

So Jasper had finally mustered himself into action and would take on Town Hall. He grabbed the tattered certificate and a handful of cash from the household savings tin and headed to his truck.

"Come on, Dog. You may as well come get your own tag and make it all official." The Dog hopped into the truck, his paws encrusted in mud from a morning run into the swamp out back. His tail was drenched and his face was covered with dirt, seeds and assorted plant material. Jasper was too anxious to notice.

The Town Hall was housed in a quaint clapboarded building in the Village. The tax office was downstairs in the made-over basement area. The town had redone the building in 1965 and had never seen their way to fixing it up any further. Heating pipes weaved across the ceiling, tangles of computer wires were duct taped to them in many spots. Ancient and buzzing florescent fixtures provided grayish light. It had all the atmosphere of an interrogation room. Recently, the selectmen had voted to install a glass security panel in the room. The town clerk, Polly Hedron had insisted that they had a disaster waiting to happen. Picture all that tax money passing across the counters, and all they would need was just *one* angry resident to vault that counter and there could be an "incident." Polly could testify that she had seen any number of highly agitated people in that office in her day and they were just playing with a loaded gun.

That was all the board needed. Each one had been the victim of a Polly stare, authoritative and humbling. They all had offered a muttered yet unwilling agreement to whatever Polly demanded at some point in their residency. Yes, indeed, security was a necessary expense this time.

The wall was a solid panel of thick, bulletproof glass. Therein lay the problem. Neally had found a good discount glass service but they had neglected to add the little speaking hole at face height for each station. There was a small opening at the bottom at each of the three stations at the counter, through which patrons could pass papers and payments. The missing holes did not seem to be a problem for Polly whose booming voice carried much farther than anyone appreciated anyway.

Jasper entered the room meekly, as a bad boy would enter the principal's office. The Dog followed along behind, much less meekly. In fact, he was alert and... *happy*. His tail wagged ferociously, sending a spray of swamp water left and right. A trail of muddy paw prints marked his course into the office, a zigzag of sniffs and licks on walls, doors and fire extinguishers. The Dog was remarkably well house-trained and at least refrained from marking a territory in the building despite all the interesting smells he encountered.

Jasper had not seen the new "wall," though he had heard plenty about it from Neally. Now he faced it, perplexed. Most people managed to carry on with their business shouting as needed to get their point across the barrier. Jasper, however found the missing hole quite disconcerting. He approached the first station tentatively. Polly waited on the other side, staring at him. He started to pass the papers from Doc through the slot then yanked them back suddenly. He sidled to the right to the middle station, studied it a bit and then worked his way over to the third station, where Polly's sister, Tetra, sat by her computer, staring at him.

"Whaddya doin' Jaspah? You want to registah

your cah? This station is just for cah registration. I can do the state or the town or both. Do you need new plates? You gotta get your sitckah's here too, ya know." Tetra paused to breath. Her rather large frame heaved slightly and she perched on the stool, snapping a piece of gum in her mouth. "So what are you doin' today, Jaspah?"

Jasper looked at her dumbfounded. He bent over slightly so that his mouth was close to the slot in the counter.

"Um, no cah today Tetra. I need to registah The Dog. Can you do that here?"

"Oh no, Jaspah. You gotta go over there and see Polly. I only do the cah stuff. I was trained 'specially for it." Tetra pointed at Polly who had reseated herself at a large paper strewn desk in the area behind the counter. She was working a tally of some sort, banging out a rhythm on her adding machine.

Jasper stepped to the middle station and bent over to speak through the slot.

"Polly? Polly, can you take this here registration for The Dog? I got a notice from you that ..."

"*Jaspah!* Dog registrations are *only* done at Station One. This station is for property taxes and dump stickahs! Can't you read the signs?" Polly shot him a look of disgust and continued her calculating.

Jasper looked left and right for a sign. He glanced below the counter and behind him. He looked up and saw nothing. Tetra waved at him and pointed up … There at the top of the glass panel he saw a yellow sticky note that read "Prop. Tax – Dump."

"Oh."

He moved left to the first station. He noticed another slip of pink paper stuck to the glass that read "Misc. Business." He slid the Doc's certificate into the slot where it was sucked away out of his reach by the large fan blowing in the corner. Polly continued to calculate. Jasper bent down to counter level to speak.

"Ahem?" he offered tentatively." Um, Polly? You work *here*?"

"Well, of *course* I am, Jaspah. I work here everyday! I'm not like the Chief and that Cal Deckland who can lounge down at the store all day! I have to work during my hours!" She huffed at him indignantly from across the large desk. The adding machine tape danced in the breeze from fan. The silence was deafening. Jasper wasn't sure what had provoked this. He did know that women were a funny sort and Polly was one of *the* toughest birds around. Still bent over the counter edge, he continued on carefully.

"Um, er, Polly, I kinda just meant are *you* working here at *this* station, cause, I, um need to registah this dog." Jasper pointed at The Dog who was shredding a Wanted poster which he had pulled down off the bulletin board, along with three public meeting notices which lay in a muddy mess beside him. At the sound of his name, The Dog, mindfully, padded over to Jasper and wagged his tail, spattering the security panel with muddy splats! Polly rose from her seat, enraged. Tetra dodged into corner mumbling that she had to copy something.

"JASPAH!! WHAT ARE YOU THINKING? THIS IS A PROFESSIONAL OFFICE, AND LOOK WHAT YOUR DOG HAS DONE!" she screeched. "Why is that animal in here? Register him? You are lucky I don't have him put in the pound for destroying government property! Do you know that wetting down that material might just be a federal offense?"

Jasper straightened a bit but he had learned long ago that Polly's questions were rarely rhetorical. He bent over and spat his reply through the slot once again.

"Welp, I figured it would be better to have him here in case you had any questions about what kind he is or what color! Polly, you can see he is not an easy fellow to define!" The Dog chose this inopportune moment to place his paws on the counter and hoist his face up level with Jasper's. The Dog sniffed excitedly through the hole leaving a ring of wet nose prints and a small pool of slobber on the surface. Jasper swiped at it with his sleeve hoping that Polly wouldn't notice.

"OH, for gawd's sake, JASPAH! Get that animal *down*" Polly swiftly produced box of tissues and some antibacterial spray cleaner from the shelf below. She squirted the glass and counter through the slot, as well as Jasper and The Dog.

The Dog launched himself flat onto the floor, wiping at his face with his paws in panic. Jasper coughed and sputtered but bravely returned to the inconveniently placed speaking slot.

"Now Polly... You didn't have to do *that*! That was just plain mean! Now get over here and let's get him registered so I can get the heck out here and leave!" He stuck his hand though the slot and wiggled his fingers at the papers which were just beyond his reach. "Please, Polly?"

Reluctantly, she pinched the edge of the papers and began to register The Dog, because for once she agreed with Jasper and knew he was right. She stepped over to her computer and began tapping at the keyboard with the speed and vengeance of a woodpecker at a good bug tree. She spaced and entered, turning each page of the documents provided by Doc Nickles. She consulted the screen, turned the pages again, and turned to Jasper, who was contorting himself into a back stretch after having hovered at counter level for last ten minutes.

"Jasper?"

"Ayah, Polly." He bent down wearily to speak.

"What is the dog's *proper* name? Doc Nickles must be losing his touch, he never does this! He didn't write in a real name. You know you're going to have to back to him and have him fill this out properly before I can process this registration! I need the dog's proper name on the rabies certificate, signed by the veterinarian. That is the law, Jasper! I know you think I make these things up but that *is* the *law*!" Polly tried to slide the papers back through but Jasper had his hands wedged across the opening.

"Polly! You are pushing me *too* far now! His name is on that paper! He is The Dog. That is his name. I ain't taking that back." Jasper risked removing one hand to grab a ten dollar bill from his pocket, and then pushed toward Polly. "Here! Here is your money. The Dog is all fixed and Doc said he is just fine."

"I don't have to registah him, if you *do not* have a name for your animal. State law says you need a name!"

"HE'S GOT A NAME! You just put "The Dog" on your computer and the state will be *happy*, I will be happy, The Dog will be happy, and you will be HAPPY because we will leave!"

Jasper lifted his head slightly and stared into the eye of the tigress through the pane. Polly and he remained locked on for several moments, neither giving an inch on their side of the barrier. They were startled when the phone on Polly's desk rang loudly.

"Tetra, get that for me please?" Polly called to her sister. "I am busy with this here just now.

Tetra grabbed the receiver and listened. She nodded and mumbled something to the caller.

"Well, who is it and what do they want, Tetra?" Annoyed, Polly twisted back toward her sister, leaving her hand across the slot, her arm bent at an uncomfortable angle. She wondered briefly if workman's comp would cover a strain or tendonitis incurred as a result of such an unnatural position and situation.

"Polly, it's Jaspah's bettah half. She wants to talk to you." Tetra stretched the curly cord to the hand piece as far as it would go to reach Polly at the counter. Polly leaned over to listen.

"Ayuh…Uh-huh…. But …I know. But…Yes. He *is* the most stubborn man I've met. I suppose. But, the name? What will the state say? I suppose. Okay. God bless you dear. That would never be allowed in *my* house, but you do as you see fit!... Yes, see you at Ladies Guild tonight. Buh-bye dear!" Polly nodded to Tetra that it was okay to hang up. She turned back to Jasper.

"Lucky for you, your lovely wife has explained how unreasonable you can be and she assured me that I could process the registration without a proper name. It seems her sister has some connections up to the State in animal registrations and will cover for me if it becomes an issue. I'll have to put an override in the section to get it to take though."

23

Polly pecked and printed and demanded rather impolitely that he sign the registration. She tore the sheaves apart and dramatically presented one to Jasper through the slot. Jasper accepted the paperwork as a conciliatory gesture and he gleamed in triumph.

Polly knew she had given in for Mother's sake. God bless her! She had this man and that animal to contend with *every* day. She took a registration tag from the box and pushed it with one finger through the slot.

"Jasper put this *on* the dog. It's not legal if you don't. *He's* not legal, if you don't!" Jasper flipped it up with one finger and caught it in mid air, grinning.

"No problem, Polly!" Jasper waved to Polly's sister then headed for the door. "Have a nice day Tetra! Come on, Dog!"

The Dog was still propped, with his paws on the counter. It twitched one huge pointed ear toward Jasper, wagged his whippy tail, thumping it left, and then right on the wall below the counter. The Dog then locked a gaze on Polly and she swore that she saw the animal smile at her, for just a flash, before it hopped down and traipsed out the door behind Jasper, both leaving a muddy trail of foot prints on her gleaming floor.

The Greens Keeper

"Well, I'm off Mothuh!" Jasper called out from the breezeway as he plopped his best Deere cap on his head. Before Mother could ask where "off" was, Jasper was spraying gravel in the driveway.

Jasper whistled a little tune as he rolled into George Hubbard's yard. It wouldn't take long could take to mow the place, he pondered. Glancing at the rough perimeters, Jasper figured on at least an hour maybe an hour and a half tops, with a break for a glass of iced tea. Then he had to figure on the post-mow, blade cleaning a sharpening. He'd need to oil it up and refill it with gas too. With a little determination,

Jasper could stretch this job over two full hours. He couldn't wait to get started.

It was quite by chance that Jasper had discovered that each Wednesday evening the field at the Village Elementary School, was the site of women's soccer matches. He had asked around a bit at the Village Store and it seems there was a league of women over thirty that played there throughout the summer. It just happened that Jasper's fishing buddy, George owned a house which abutted the school yard. George and his wife, Melinda had a seasonal reservation for their camper up in north at a campground, they took off come summer and only returned to check up on the yard every few weeks.

George and Mel had hosted a send off cookout for themselves, inviting Jasper and Mother for burgers and beers. The couples settled themselves out on the screen porch out back.

"Well, Mel, you must be excited to be off to the lake this year. Eh? Do you have everything packed?" Mother inquired in between bites of substantial burger. "Excuse me dear, what did you say?"Mel cupped her ear with one hand. Beyond them, in the field several dozen women in shorts and tank tops were assembling. They were calling encouragement and shouting directions to one another as they kicked a black and white ball. Jasper sat up attentively. There was one man out there, blowing his whistle and running about among the women.

Jasper ambled out the door announcing that he needed to "check out George's yard". He dragged George from his dinner and insisted that he should come show him the property lines.

They stood out there talking about mostly nothing, that George could figure, while casually observing the game.

"So what's this game all about George?" Jasper fished.

"Dunno exactly. They come up here every Wednesday practically and chase that ball around. They think its fun, I guess. Some of them women even change their shirts out there right in front of every one.... Mel says it's okay. They wear that sports underwear, which is more than most women wear at the beach, but it sure seems weird to me. So what are you're plans for the summer Jasper?" George turned to Jasper and realized he was not going to receive any kind of clear answer. Jasper's eyes were glazed over as he stood mesmerized by the women running to and fro on the field in front of them.

Then suddenly, Jasper broke from his reverie.

"You know George; I bet you need some help 'round here this summer. You know I got that super John Deere for my yahd last year and I could zip over here in flash and have your yard done for you. It's got to be a real pain to have to wonder how long the grass is getting here when you are up at the camp." Jasper offered benevolently. George was stunned silent. Jasper never did anything without some sort of angle behind it.

"Uh...um…Why, Jasper that's really nice of you to offer. But are you sure that you want to take this on? I mean we have a good acre and a half of lawn here. It can be beastly to mow in the summer … hot as heck in the day and all the bugs at night, you know." George looked him dubiously.

"Of course, George, I have always felt badly that you had to tote yourself all the way back down here to tend to the place." Jasper smiled magnanimously. "I tell you what. I'll take care of your lawn and maybe you can have Mothuh up to your camp for a bit this summer. She loves to get up there and go to the outlets, and she has that jet ski thing too. So whaddya think? We gotta deal?"

"Errr, sure, Jasper that would be fine. Mel would love to have her up and she actually has been dying to try out that jet ski."

The deal was sealed and Jasper was as excited as a little boy waiting for Christmas. George and Melinda were fairly befuddled when on the morning of their departure for camp; Jasper arrived with two cups of Dunkin Donuts coffee from all the way in town and helped them haul the last of their luggage into the car. As they drove away, Mel glanced back.

"George! GEORGE! Stop the car....I think Jasper's having a seizure!" She grabbed his arm and he slowed the vehicle to a stop and took a look back.

"Mel! You gotta calm yourself! And put down that cell phone! Jasper does not need help from 911." George turned back to the wheel and put the car back into gear.

"But dear, didn't you see him. He was thrashing all about the driveway. Somethin's wrong with him!"

George sighed loudly.

"Jasper was doing some sort of jig. I haven't a clue why but I believe he's dancing! He *can* be a strange sort of coot sometimes." With that he accelerated off to camp, leaving his lawn care worries behind him for the summer.

On the very next Wednesday evening, Jasper was over at the Hubbard's house ready to mow at six o'clock sharp. He waited out by the side of the garage. He could see a bit of the field and the parking lot and could keep an eye on when the players started to arrive. He had a cooler of cold Budweiser ready in the rack on the back of the Deere. He had spent the better part of the afternoon rigging up this basket which was duct taped to the back of his seat. He had done a few test runs with some soda cans in the afternoon and had determined the perfect reach radius. Now, he could drive comfortably and enjoy some refreshment without stopping.

Jasper surveyed they yard carefully. He knew that he needed to maximize his time out in the back yard, yet not be too obvious. He started by turning some wide curly-q's as the women started out to the field. He felt the looped pattern would be the most forgiving, as his focus was elsewhere than the grass directly in front of him. He estimated his speed at less than 5 miles per hour. This allowed him to drive with pinky finger control on the steering wheel, giving him a casual yet controlled look. He set off, his best John Deere cap tilted back on his head a jaunty angle.

The game began within minutes and the women took little notice of Jasper initially. They ran up and down the white lined field chipping the white and black ball among them. Now and then the ball would hit the chain link fence around the field with a loud "CHINNNKK!" which made Jasper jump in his seat just a bit, and slow to a turtle's pace while he watched a woman race off the field, grab the ball and toss it with hands over her head, into the mass of womanhood milling about in front of her. He heard the tweet of the whistle from the only man in sight, some tight bummed fellow in little black pants.

"Hmm, now that's a job...though meddling rules between twenty some women really ain't such and enviable position for any man.... And, any guy wearing those tiny little pants just ain't right!" Jasper mumbled to himself.

Eventually he had to make a pass out to the front yard. Jasper picked up speed noticeably and mowed the front yard in a record time. He headed out back again, leaving tufty streaks of tall grass all over the yard behind him.

Jasper heard a loud, long double whistle over the putt of his engine and noticed that all the women were running off the field, to plop down on the grass right in front of the Hubbards' yard! Jasper mowed casually to the back corner by the fence threw it into reverse for second without applying the clutch, and the mower made a short but shrill bark. He turned off the engine and hopped off wearing his concerned but in control demeanor. He casually waved to the women who had been temporarily silenced by the noise, then reached into his cooler for a can of Budweiser.

"Can I offer any of you ladies a cool one?" Jasper called over the fence as he casually popped the top and leaned with one arm on the fence. The beer having been bounced around on the back of the tractor for the better part of the hour, immediately exploded in a stream of foam right into Jasper's face.

A ripple of quiet laughter that flowed through the assembly, but Jasper recovered, retrieving a red bandanna out of the back pocket of his overalls.

"Heh, that's one way to cool off I suppose!" he announced to the gathering.

The women had turned away as the man in the tight little black shorts was whistling them into the field again. With one last swipe of their glistening faces and chests heaving a deep breath, the women of Jasper's mowing fantasy ran away in their tiny shorts. Jasper restarted his mower and began to work a patchwork pattern that would have made the greens keeper at Fenway Park envious. He zigged and zagged and looped and crossed, all the while keeping one eye on the bouncing bounty of womanhood that jogged before him on that green tableau.

The best moment of the evening came a few minute into the second half when a lady in the back field, sent the ball arching into the sky and over the fence into George's flower bed. A woman ran to the fence and waved to Jasper.

"Sir? Would you mind getting our ball?" Her chest heaved from the exertion of the game.

Jasper was mesmerized, had to shake himself into action. He threw the mower into neutral and hopped off the tractor and ran to the flower bed. A few feet from the raised edge he launched himself into a high hurdle jump over the flowers. In high school he had been quite the dashing athlete, tackling hurdles on the track with the ease and agility of a young gazelle. Unfortunately for Jasper, the four beers he had consumed during his mowing experience and his not so young, not so athletic self now landed, butt first, on Mel's prize Heritage Rose bush.

At this point every eye on the field was watching him. He rolled around like Winnie the Pooh stuck in his hunny pot.

"Gawd-DAMMMITTT! GAAAAAWD dam - it- ALLL! Oomph!" Jasper rolled right then left, arching up over the stray ball on his belly. The ball rolled out from under him instantly and landed him face first in Mel's "special manure mix" compost mulch.

It was then he heard the click of sensible shoes across the Hubbard's concrete patio. His eyes sealed shut with compost; he sensed a familiarly formidable presence nearing. Mother reached over his bony behind, grabbed the ball and drop kicked it over the fence to the waiting athlete.

"Jasper, what are you doing in this garden?" Mother hissed at him. "And what have you done to George's yard? The grass has been cut down to nothing and there are tufts of long stuff all over the front. Jasper sat up, wiping the manure mix from his face with his bandanna. He looked up at Mother then, even though he knew it was a mistake, even though he knew he would pay for his actions ever so dearly... he glanced out at the field as the sun dropped into a red glow in the sky, silhouetting the players on the field, female figures shrouded in a golden glow, and then he sighed, spitting a bit of dirt from his lips as he did.

"Well, get up, you donkey!" Mother gave his overall strap a yank and hauled him to his feet. "You just get yourself home and wash up. I'll clean up here and bring home the Deere. You take my car, but, mind you don't get any manure mix on my upholstery!"

Jasper untangled himself from the thorny branches that had locked onto his legs, and stumbled off, his head drooping, his feet dragging.

Epilogue:

Mother re-scheduled Jasper's extracurricular mowing for the balance of the summer. He was allowed to mow only on Tuesday mornings.

Mother, as a result of her strong return kick, had been asked to play with the local team, which, though she was honored by the invitation, she turned down.

George and Mel returned from vacation and presented Jasper with a bag of Mel's Special manure mix, but were quite confused when Jasper refused to accept. He mumbled something about having had enough fertilizer for the summer and they should just keep their manure to themselves.

Jasper never volunteered to groom the Hubbard's yard again, and to this day, Mel has never

understood why her Heritage Rose is slightly droopy
on one side.

Her Day

Mother looked at Jasper with particular disgust. He was used her moods and often planned his day according to which look he received. He approached her cautiously, mumbling incoherently, as he staggered about trying to pour himself a cup of coffee. Jasper didn't know what it was that he had done this time, but on the mean and ugly scale, Mother was hitting a high nine this morning.

"Mu-rumhin'." he mumbled in her direction.

All he got from her a sigh of sorts, long and slow, like the air was being let out of a tire from a tiny pinhole under tremendous pressure.

37

He thought he better speak up because it seemed to him that she was going to blow It was peculiar though, as Mother, generally tolerated almost all his schemes, opinions and goings on with an unreasonable amount of patience.

"Well, ain't it a beautiful day, Mother?" Jasper tugged the curtain aside to reveal a gray, dismal sky. He tried a slightly different approach and continued on with a forged air of cheerfulness, "Well Mother, is that what's bothering you now?...Well, a little damp weather will be just the thing for your garden! May is the time for those little pee-OH-knees to grow. The forsickias are looking chipper too!" For Jasper, this was down right sweet as honey and he hated himself but it would be hell around the house if he didn't find out what was wrong with Mother quick.

He grinned his best rough and tumble "boy" look (a look perfected in his youth but honed carefully to accommodate the crinkles of age into his act.) Still, her gaze was as steely and gray as the threatening spring sky but the kettle started to whistle with boiling water for her cup of tea, and she momentarily broke her laser lock look on Jasper.

Not one to lose an opportunity, Jasper scampered as only a man in trouble could, silently as smoke, out the door.

He called to her from the yard in a falsetto of affected cheerfulness. "You know, deah...I think I will just go down to the store and see if the mail's in!" Mother heard the truck door slam and the scritch of the tires on the gravel driveway, as he peeled out of the yard.

"Fool man! It's seven in the morning and the mail truck doesn't arrive till at least eight thirty...I should've just kicked him first thing, and been done with it."

When he got to the Crooked Rd, Jasper thought it was safe to slow up a bit especially in case Ed was out on patrol. He didn't want to give the Chief an excuse to charge breakfast to his account. He dawdled through the twists, irritating some "yupster" in one of those foreign cars that tagged along behind his rusty truck. Jasper could hear the fancy engine racing, and in his side view mirror, he could glimpse the contortion of rage building in the driver's face.

"Well, now, guess I bettah' be sure that I'm driving safely now!" And Jasper slowed to fifteen miles an hour. He found it fun to sport a bit with an impatient pinhead. He turned in at the Village Store and waved cheerfully to the other driver. The man in response waved with only one finger then accelerated out of sight.

Inside the store, Jasper hailed the regulars, though most were surprised to see him there so early.

"Did ya see that pinhead? Idiot man in his foreign tuna can! Them SAB's don't hold a candle to my truck.

"Well, I didn't see that, but I do see a pinhead right in front of me!" Ed Peterson, the chief of police bellowed across the room. At the small table with him was Neally Kendall, the head of the selectmen and Cal Deckland who was the local road agent.

"What the hell you doing here so dang-nable early, Jasper? You aren't due here for another half hour!" Cal punctuated his question with a loud slurpy sip of coffee from a plastic mug that was dirtier than the bed of Jasper's truck.

"Aww, Jay-sus! Mother's having a day! Meaner than a skunk who's woke up too early! Thought it was safer to lay low here for a bit till she warms up."

"When'll that be, Jasper, next September?" Neally chuckled from behind his newspaper.

"What the heck did ya do this time, Jasper? I thought you knew better than to haul manure in her car?." Cal sucked the jelly out of his donut loudly.

"I dunno. I've been going over it all in my head. Yesterday was Sunday. She went to church as usual. I stayed home and read the newspaper. She came back and seemed fine. She made a great dinner, I watched the ballgame while she did the dishes, just like always…she always enjoys her time alone in the kitchen - I never mess with that!" Jasper took a seat at the table and waved to Noreen for an egg muffin. He hadn't had time to get his "regular" bowl of shredded wheat and that alone could ruin a whole day for him.

"So what else did you do yesterday? You must of done something. Maybe you should've helped her out in the kitchen or somethin'" Cal wiped a stripe of jelly from his greasy t-shirt and licked it off an equally greasy finger with an expression of complete satisfaction.

"Nope. She hates it when I go messing around in the kitchen. She says I never put anything back in the right place." Jasper winked at Neally. "Of course, I never have made much effort to learn where the stuff goes. It only makes sense to me not to."

"Now after that I had a nap, we had a little cereal for snack and was off to bed by nine...." Jasper sighed with the effort of the explanation. "So what did you do yesterday?"

Cal smiled. "I made sure I got up early and washed the Blazer. Me and the girls took the wife out for the bruncheon buffet at the Wander Inn up to Concord. She loved it. The girls had made cards at school so she was happy most of the day. I worked on the backhoe all afternoon, but Bethy was so full of bacon and tater tots, that I couldn't do anything wrong!"

"Well, I made sure I got a boo-kay at that Walmart Super Center on Saturday for the wife!" added Ed. "She always loves flowers. We drove over to her mother's and ate there yesterday. I hate that women's cooking but, I figure, it's only once a year."

He folded his newspaper and slapped it authoritatively on the sticky table.

"Whaaat?" Jasper looked from one to the other with a sense of panic. "What comes once a year?"

"Why Mothuh's Day, of course, Jasper!" Noreen cracked him on the head with her knuckle and slid his egg muffin on a folding paper plate onto the table, then continued on without taking a breath. "Catch this before it falls, will ya? I had to work here of course but Kelly brought the kids over…They love the egg-muffins too. Anyway, they were here till I was off at 2 and then we went for a drive to Hampton, of course. You know, down the arcade? I jest love to play ski ball! Did I tell you I used to be a champ? Got first place once in 1983…..."

"Err, Yeah Noreen. We've all heard it before… Look you have customer at the register, hon." Neally redirected her and she launched her monologue on Mrs. Dobbins who tried, admirably, to buy just a small tube of antacids.

"Yesterday was Mothuh's Day?" Jasper looked stunned.

"Ay-uh "

"Uh-oh."

"A-yuh." Neally confirmed. "Looks like you got troubles Jasper!"

"Ay-uh!"

"So what you gonna do, Jasper?" Cal wiped his mouth with the edge of his t-shirt sleeve and threw his unused paper napkin into a nearby wastebasket.

"Hey, two points for me! Gotta love that! I coulda played professionally, ya know?"

"I dunno. I gotta make a plan. I gotta move out a here though. Mother will have those biddies from her garden club down here in a bit just to make my life miserable." sighed Jasper.

"You want the key to the shed at the dump so you can hide out? I gotta take a mess of bumps out of the Crooked Road today, otherwise I'd go fishin' or wander up to the taxidermy with ya." Cal slid off his seat and shuffled over to the register to settle up with Noreen.

"Nope. Don't need the key. I gotta figure out how to get myself out of this jam. Thanks anyway, though, Cal." Jasper mumbled as he wandered out to his truck.

Now Jasper had been in fixes before but Mother never had been that steely with him. He had to come up with something really special to get him out of this stew. As he drove out onto the highway, he headed up to the city. Then it hit him- *the Mall*! That was it. Mother loved the mall. They didn't go up there often. Jasper hated the Mall. It was just weird. The kids all dressed so strange up there. Jasper couldn't help staring. Jasper pulled into the Mall and circled interminably till he saw the light of salvation - the SEARS sign, glowing like a message from heaven.

"By gawry, that's where I gotta go! Mother just loves anything that Ty Pencilton does on that Extreme Makeover TV show! He works for Sears. I've seen him on the commercials! That man's gonna save my butt!" He parked and headed into the store.

Jasper, by instinct, turned left and headed toward the tool department. It was a lure he couldn't resist. Most of Jasper's tools, despite his better intentions, seem to be massed in a grubby tangle in his shed. Here, they were clean and so beautiful. He stalled in the aisle, mouth gaping, staggered by the shiny display. There were *so* many power tools, hammers, oh, and drills, too many to count! A curl of drool was on the brink of dribbling down his chin, when he was yanked suddenly back to reality.

"Good afternoon sir. Welcome to Sears! Is there something I can help you with this fine morning? Perhaps you might be interested in a cordless drill, set of bits, or a new chainsaw? You look like a man of the outdoors!"

Jasper, in his stained and worn every day work clothes, turned dumbfounded toward the chipper young man who had addressed him.

"By gawd, he must be one of those prodigies." thought Jasper.

"You son, *can* help. You are right! Absolutely right! A chainsaw would be just the thing." Jasper read the salesman's nametag. "Kyle, is it? Why, you are some smart fella!"

"Yes sir! Why don't you follow me down to aisle N to check out our new models? We have a nice selection, even couple on sale for a reasonable price...." Kyle kept selling as he turned up the next aisle, and Jasper followed along like a dog after a boy with a tasty biscuit.

He saw the fancy displays and knew it might be hard to choose if he should allow himself to become distracted by the finely crafted cases, and shimmering sets of notched blades. He shook his head to clear it. Stick to business now mister, he told himself.

"I need a nice little saw, a pretty one that a lady would like. Hmmm, that little green one over there looks fine. In fact I believe green is Mothuh's favorite color... I think." Jasper finished in a mumble.

"Why, that, sir, is a efficient little model, perhaps a tad small for you but..." Jasper lost his focus on Kyle at that moment, as he felt relief course through his body. Mother will love this! He was saved. He nodded to Kyle and slipped a wad of cash from his overall pocket.

"So Kyle, how about you ring this one up and how about you give me a nice bag or something for it? Do you think that CVS down there in the mall would have any Mothuh's Day cards left?... How about you set that aside whilst I go see if I can find a nice one?" Jasper fairly skipped toward the exit, leaving Kyle still talking about the varied options available to him for service.

"Ahh, yes..sir?..... Thank you for shopping at Sears....?"

Mother sat at the kitchen table. The morning sun was fading and she had vented most of her ire by cleaning the entire house, restacking a cord of wood and re-organizing Jasper's tool shed. He had no sense of where to put things so she had disposed, sorted and stored everything according to her system. She smiled with satisfaction. This time, Jasper deserved it.

She had started to heat up some hot dogs and beans for lunch when she heard the truck in the yard. Jasper was driving carefully, which meant to her that he was up to something....again.

He was grinning wider than a clown at the Barnum circus when he sidled up to the back door. The screen door creaked open and Jasper greeted her sweet as butterscotch.

"Well how are you this fine day, my darling?"

Mother stared at him in disbelief.

"Well, now it seems that I forgot something awful important and I have gotten you somethin' extra special to make up for it."

46

"Yes." Mother's eyes still had the glint of steel, stainless steel, in them.

Jasper forged on.

"Ayuh. Here it is." He crept out the door and slid in again with a giant blue plastic sack. It hit the table with a solid thud.

Mother had to admit that her curiosity was piqued.

"This is for me?"

"Ayuh. I even had Kyle at the Sears put it in a fancy bag for you. They don't do *that* for everyone, ya know. He thinks it's one of them Ty Pencilton editions. And I got you this too." Jasper handed her a card. "Now I tried to get one of those nice flowery cards for you Mothuh, but that damnable woman at the CVS had pulled all the cards this morning and she wouldn't give me one no matter how much I begged. I even offered to pay seventy-five percent of the price. Heck, the holiday is done, they should have *given* it to me and help them empty out the trash. Anyway, she didn't wanna, so I got this one because it looked pretty...don't ya think? I thought you'd like the flowers on front."

Mother read the card aloud.

"*My deepest sympathy at your time of loss...?*"

"Don't ya love them flowers though, Mother?... and the fancy gold swirly letters...They 'boss them on there, ya know!" Jasper added quickly, waiting for Mother's glowing look of forgiveness.

47

It didn't come.

"Ah, hum, well, um, how about you open your present?" He dropped the bag her feet with a thump. He was having second thoughts about the wisdom of giving her a cutting instrument of any kind when she was in such a mood.

Mother leaned over and unstapled the bag.

"Kyle did a lovely wrapping job, don't ya think?" Jasper cringed. She sure wasn't making it easy for him. What did a man have to do to dig himself out trouble? Before he could sink into the well of self-pity, he heard mother sigh appreciatively.

She had withdrawn the shiny case and popped the plastic locks.

"Oooooooooh…" she whispered as she withdrew the bright green saw. "Well, Jasper, maybe you aren't the entire idiot you seem to be…I assume that it's oiled and gassed and ready to go?"

"Ayuh…um, yep. Kyle took care of me…er,…yeah, of course I took care of it for you, darlin'." Jasper fumbled with a coffee cup, avoiding Mother's stare. "Maybe you oughta try it out?"

Mother hefted the saw over her shoulder and headed toward the yard. As she passed Jasper, who had turned to pour his coffee, he felt the slightest pat on his backside.

"Ah, she still thinks I'm somethin'!" Jasper was forgiven and content, as he heard the whine of wood being cut in the yard.

Grandparents Day

Jasper settled into his recliner with a creak. He sprayed open a can of beer with a pinch of the flip top. Jasper sighed with satisfaction. It had been an interminably long day. There was nothing finer than retiring to his favorite chair with its cushion broken perfectly to his bony behind.

Today had been Grandparents Day at the Village school. Mother and Jasper had never been "blessed" with their own children. This was fine with Jasper. He enjoyed comfort, solitude and silence. However, Mother had a nephew, Chuckie who was eight years old. She indulged him as she would a grandchild.

Her little sister, Martha, had married late   after 12 years in a career with the state up at the toll booth on Route 93. She had even earned the honor of "Best Token Catcher" for the entire state for six years in a row! Then when she hit her late thirties, Jasper assumed that she had heard that clock on her reproductive urges ticking and she and her slug of a husband had reproduced. Chuckie- who was actually "Charles Elvis" who was named for Martha's favorite royalty- Prince Charles, and the King of rock and roll.

Jasper thought that Chuckie was an okay kid, but he could tolerate him only in small doses . Chuckie was a "high energy" child (as described by Mother who tended to have a more generous spirit). Jasper knew they had some fancy letter names for   it; H.A.D.I.T. or something like that; He could never remember. All he knew was that Chuckie was a little hellion who rarely listened. Martha dropped him off at the house often, so that she could go out on a "date" with her creep of a husband, Crandall.

"The man is a *moron*, Mothuh! I can't talk to him about *nothin'*!" Jasper would exclaim. "Why, he don't even read the Letters to the Editor! How did she end up with such a turkey?"

Mother would simply smile and reply:

"Well, I don't know about that, dear."

Mother liked Crandall. He was a quiet guy who also worked for the State as a tax auditor. He traveled a bit and Mother was more than happy to help Martha with Chuckie. Since Martha had retired from the tollbooth she had been thrilled to finally be a mother, but had always felt the loss of her career. She felt that she had been on track for a promotion to Exit Seven Assistant Supervisor with, perhaps a future at the state office in the Department of Accounting and Justification.

Little Chuckie's arrival had changed that for her and now she owned a small ceramics business based in her breezeway. She also attended weekly fitness session at the park and rec, to keep herself in top "token catching"condition so she could perhaps return to the booth again in a few years. Both these ventures somehow increased the time Mothuh volunteered to watch her little 'darlin', much to Jasper's dismay.

When the subject of Grandparents Day had come up over coffee, Martha had asked Mother to attend for "Chuckie's sake." It was so hard on him not having a grandparent nearby...or alive, for that matter. Unfortunately, the date was the same as the Women's Guild's annual Outlet Marathon, so Mother had volunteered Jasper to attend.

As codgety as Jasper was, he knew that he couldn't disappoint Chuckie. Besides, he knew that if he didn't go, Mother would make his life hell on Earth.

So there he was, driving into the schoolyard, trying to ignore that old belly ache he always got when he approached the place.

Going to school had always been a test of Jasper's patience but Grandparents Day was to be the final exam.

A large banner hung from the front of the building which read "WELCOME!!! Let's have a GRAND Day!!

Jasper sighed, then growled. "Grand, my butt." And he threw his clutch into reverse with a grind. He created quite a stir among the visitors gathered out front as he wedged his rusty, old pickup into a spot with a persistent "beep-beep-beep" of the shrill back up alarm piercing the quiet of the morning. Mother had protested that the alarm was excessively loud and completely unnecessary, but Jasper had insisted that it had saved him from running down any number of brainless twerps down at the dump. Mother would then correct Jasper firmly, 'Jasper it's a 'recycling' center," which he would promptly ignore.

He noticed that several of the 'grands' were clutching their chests with relief when he shut of the engine and kicked his door shut. He cut through the crowd and stepped up front to t h e cheerfully decorated table and several equally cheerful volunteer helpers.

"So where's Chuckie?" he asked abruptly.

"Welcome sir! If you would please check your name off our list and then I can make you a name tag, um, Mister....?" She poised her cheery green marker over a label adorned with daisies and butterflies.

"Name's Jasper. And I won't need one those sissy sassy tags."

"Well, ahh, Mr. Jasper, everyone must wear an ID in our school, in case of an emergency situation. You understand of cours..." Her spiel was cut short.

"Nope. Don't need one. Don't need everyone knowing me if they haven't bothered to know me by now." Jasper scowled at the woman.

"Well, Mr... um, Jasper we do need to follow school rules so here you go." The smiley woman tentatively slid the label across the table toward him.

"Nope. You know who I am now, right? I know who I am and Chuckie knows who I am and I kinda figure that's plenty of people nosing around in my bizness." Jasper took a deep breath, slightly winded, unused to speaking at such length. "So where do I find Chuckie?"

"Chuckie?"

"Yep. Chuckie Elvis Stockdale."

She reached for fat computer list in front of a blonde who was definitely not natural, and riffled through the pages.

"Ahh, here he is....You want Miss Feinhaus' room which is 3F. You just go with that group over there. 'Strawberry' Christine will be you guide" She pointed to a woman by the hall doors who was wearing giant strawberry shaped cardboard hat.

"Jeez-um-crow-Mike." mumbled Jasper as the volunteer gratefully dismissed him with a wave.

Jasper joined the strawberry "jam" in the corner, ignoring the constant chitter from the fruity headed woman. When they started down the hall at last, he trailed along sullenly. He continued to growl to himself.

"Gawd. Mothuh is gonna owe me in a big way. I 'spect that I'll be out fishing *all* weekend!" Thinking about this made Jasper feel a lot more chipper and he actually smiled at a tottering lady next to him, whose hair was a light shade of purple.

"Here we are everyone!" Sing-Song-Sally-Strawberry waved them through, pushing Jasper into the room by closing the door on his behind.

There on the floor in a circle, were a horde of Chuckies and Chuckettes who gazed blankly at them. A tall woman in a denim jumper and the ugliest shoes he had ever seen - round toed, flat- uglier even than Mother's sensible shoes. Amazingly, she was wearing pink knee high socks covered with blue and green cartoon cats . The woman began ordering the group into seats around the room.

"Hello and welcome everyone. I am Miss Feinhaus and we are so glad that you could join us today! Class?"

The class bellowed in unison.

"WELCOME TO 3F!" Their volume caused several of the grands to wince visibly and Jasper was sure he saw at least two of them reach surreptitiously to turn down their hearing aids Miss Feinhaus called them to attention again.

"We will begin our day with our morning meeting. Would everyone please stand and join us in saying the Pledge of Allegiance."

All the grands rose respectfully from the rather tiny chairs, but not without a few muffled groans. Jasper was pleased to see that the kids seemed to actually know the pledge. He saw Chuckie waving to him fiercely. Jasper nodded his head in acknowledgment as they all began to recite.

With more scraping of chairs, the grands re-perched themselves again. Most of the children sat quietly and attentively... except for Chuckie. He sat (which was remarkable for him, in Jasper's opinion,) but with his head hanging straight back. His tongue was out and he looked he was trying to lick the head of the child next to him!

Miss Fienhaus was asking the kids about the calendar and they had begun to count the number of school days they had attended so far, which apparently was well over a thousand, because Jasper drifted off in the middle of the count. His head nodded and but awakened with a start when the teacher called out shrilly.

"CHUCKIE STANFORD! Please stop spitting in Sara's hair. That is not acceptable behavior! "

Jasper blinked his eyes to bring them into focus and saw that, indeed Chuckie was mid-spit, aiming at the little brown haired girl next to him. Chuckie quickly swallowed and glanced over at Jasper.

Now Jasper was in a pickle. He knew that he should do something disapproving but what. He usually left this kind of stuff to Mother. He furrowed his brow and growled in what he thought was Chuckie's direction. This, apparently, was not the right choice.

Miss Feinhaus addressed the class sternly. *"Boys and girls!* This is a special day and I am really disappointed that I have had to stop twice for silly behavior. Mr. Stanford! I do not expect you to growl like a wild animal in our classroom! Do you need to take a break outside in the hall?"

Chuckie at this point was studying the streaks in the linoleum flooring. "Huh? Um, Uh... No, Ms. Feinhaus! I'll be good. I'm sorry!" though he had not a clue for what he apologized.

Jasper squirmed in his seat. The gray haired church lady in the row in front of him turned on him, glaring.

"How nice! You let that poor little child

take the blame for you   rudeness!   You should be ashamed!" She huffed indignantly.

Her husband, who Jasper was sure had taken at least a box or two of Grecian Formula to that   slick head of his, pulled her closer to him and away from Jasper.

"Ya' old biddy... mind your own bizness..." he hissed soft as could be so only she and he heard it. It was then that he realized that the entire room was watching him. Miss Feinhaus sighed and then plowed on with her circle work.

The meeting broke up finally and the children were asked to go greet their grand-guests and show them around the classroom. Chuckie approached two other grands in error before he locked in on Jasper.

"Uncle   Jaspah!!!   HERE   I   AM!"   Chuckie hollered from across the room, and then ran, full speed, nearly tumbling into one older man and several of his class mates..

"Unky you gotta come see our snake! He's right here. He's cool! He eats mice – WHOLE!" he squealed loudly. Jasper noted with satisfaction that   several of the grand-dames glanced nervously around the room looking for the reptile.

At this point, Chuckie had leaped across   the room and deftly removed the cover to the snake tank with one hand and the latch for the mice cage with the other. In an instant, the room seemed to be filled with a small flood of squeaking mice. Chuckie had the snake in his hand and was waving it at another boy's elderly visitor, who was a prisoner for the show, as she was perched behind her walker, totally immobilized with fear.

The children ran screaming, chasing down small white mice, which actually numbered eight but looked like much, much more as they darted around the desks chairs and feet. Several men and women stood on the chairs and tables, while others tottered out the door into the hall. Above it all Jasper could hear Miss Feinhaus calling out in a practical but ineffective tone.

"Boys! Girls! Stop please! If you can hear me, clap once!.... If *you can hear me....*" Her voice was drowned out in the ocean of noise.

Jasper pursed his lips and issued a shrill whistle. Everyone in the room (except the mice) stopped in their tracks. As he whistled, Jasper deftly scooped the snake from Chuckie's hand and plopped it into the tank. He located Miss Feinhaus, who was on her knees, stuffing mice into her jumper pocket.

"Missy,er, Fine-ass? You want to tell me when and where I can get a coffee. I am getting quite peckish."

Miss Fienhaus reached up with her mouse hand and pointed to Chuckie. "Take *him out...NOW*... um, to the caf. Chuckie, maybe you can show Mister, um,... your grandpa where the office is?" she gestured toward the door, waving a poor mouse about over her head. She smiled just as sweet as saccharine at Jasper and he knew that look. It was a woman look and it meant business. And he knew he had better take Chuckie away for a bit, right now.

Jasper grabbed a handful of t-shirt and propelled Chuckie into the hall.

"Unky Jasper? Did you have fun? We can go down to the caf now 'cause Auntie told me to sign you up for lunch. You know what we're having today? It's the BEST one but the line is always long because all the kids really love waffles! Don't you love them, Unky J.? The syrup is *so* much better than that stuff you all have at your house out of the jugs. This syrup is sweeeeeet and really thick. You know what else they give us? Sausage patties!! Usually the kids give me theirs because most of them don't like them... but I like to stack them up and eat 'em eight at a time! It's so cool because they jus barely fit in my mouth and Susie Parnell *always* gets grossed out and sometimes she even pukes!"

At this point Chuckie actually paused for a brief few seconds to take a breath and Jasper reached over and clamped his hand over Chuckie's mouth.

"Chuckie? It looks like we're closing in on the cafeteria now. Where's the bathroom? I really need to take a pee now."

Chuckie pointed to a pale blue door frame down the hall. Jasper eased his hand off the boy's mouth and darted into the boy's room. Unfortunately, they had wandered into the primary grades and when Jasper turned the corner into the bathroom he was faced with the shortest urinals he had ever seen. The lower edge barely cleared his knees.

"Oh my Gawd! I hope my aim is still good" Jasper was still talking himself through the knee high challenge when he heard a flush. He glanced over his shoulder expecting to see a door open, but nothing happened. He waited, then finished his "bizness" and zipped. He heard a door unlatch and a tiny child with very long hair crept out of a stall. Jasper hit a small panic that he had, in fact, entered the wrong bathroom somehow. Being found in the little girl's room on grandparent's day was sure to get all over town and he would hear about it for years!

"Hey kid?" The child looked up at him shaking as he clung to the wall trying to slide by Jasper. "What are you any way?"

"Um, I-I-I'm s-six. I-I-I go to f-f-first g-g-grade." The kid screeched and escaped out the door.

Jasper bent to wash his hands at the tiny little sink, and then hurried out to find Chuckie. The boy was dangling from sprinkler head with one hand.

"Hey Unky? Look, I'm a monkey! Ya know we studied 'em in bi-homes last month. I LOVE monkeys, don't you Unky? Ya know wha…."

"*Chuckie!*" Jasper tugged on his waist and hauled him down. "Chuckie! Are you *sure* that was the men's room? Who was that little kid with the hair that just ran out? Was it a girl? Gawd help me, Chuckie, if it was ….! "

"Aw, Unky J, of course that's the boy's room! Didn't you see the funerals for us boys to pee on in there? Unk? Huh? Didn't ya?" Chuckie pulled Jasper's pant leg so that they sagged lower than was appropriate for a man Jasper's age.

"So that kid was a boy? Geez 'em, that kid needs a haircut! Why do they have to confuse me like that anyway?"

"Unky J, it's lunch time! Let's go get some food!"

Chuckie grasped Jasper's hand and dragged him toward the sickly sweet scent of very bad "genuine imitation maple syrup." In the caf, he followed Chuckie's lead and lined up to grab a cardboard tray and some plastic silverware. He watched Chuckie step up to a cloud bank of steam from which a plastic gloved hand appeared clutching a pair of nubby disks.

"Look Unky J.! WAFFLES!! YES, YES, YES! LOTSO syrup for me, PUH-LEASE, Mrs. Gonic!"

The hand pulled back and re-emerged with a ladle full of brown gooey ooze.

Chuckie stepped to the left and presented to his tray to a woman who had another smaller brown nubby disk in her hand. This tray did not steam. In fact the disks seemed stone cold.

"SAUSAGE, puh-leassse, Mrs.Narwall?" Chuckie held up his little brown disk and addressed Jasper. "Unky J., do you want your sausage? Cuz if you don't, I'll take it. I get everyone's. I like to have a lot because then I burp a lot during reading time after lunch....Hey, Unky, do sausages make you burp? You know....like this..."

Chuckie then swallowed a mouthful of air and emitted a full belly burp that rumbled through the slight child. Jasper *was* impressed. The kid had some talents.

Unfortunately, the head lady with the hairnet was not and she glowered at Chuckie. But somehow when she addressed them, she seemed to hold Jasper responsible for the faux pas.

"Chuckie! Take your tray over to the milks and help your grandfather with his lunch! And, *stop that burping!*" The towering woman waved them along. Jasper looked down and noticed that somehow, without his permission, his tray had been filled with the same nubby brown disks that Chuckie had. He followed the boy and leaned down into a large refrigerator. They each came up with a paper carton of drink. They exited to the main lunch room, where Jasper's ears were accosted with noise.

"*Holy geez!...*"Jasper's words were lost in the din. Chuckie waved him over to a table full of kids and white hairs.

They each took a seat on a small attached stool. Jasper leaned over on the table and immediately adhered to its surface. Syrup. He peeled his arm up and attacked his meal.

Now, Jasper was not a picky eater. He ate steamed hot dogs of undetermined age at the store almost every day. This substance on his tray did not appear to be edible. He stuck the fork tines into the smaller disk and reached for a knife to cut it with.

"Chuckie I need a knife. Where do I get one?"

"Unky they don't let us have knives in school. It'd be waaaay too dangerous! You should just eat it with your fingers like I do." Chuckie dangled the sausage circle from a pair of greasy, dirty fingers.

"Ayuh. Here ya' go." Jasper flipped the patty onto Chuckie's tray and turned his attention to his "waffle."

With a tap of his fork he determined that it was no softer than the tray. Jasper, used to real maple syrup, noticed that the sticky goo on his serving could be a decent substitute for epoxy. The "waffle" was now rock hard, despite its recent steaming. Jasper peeled it back from the tray and turned it over onto Chuckie's tray.

"Wow, Chuckster. You need to finish that!" Jasper unfolded himself from the stool and headed for the waste barrel. He grabbed the milk carton from his tray before pitching it and popped it open at the seam. He tipped it up and gulped down the liquid, expecting white milk, he gasped and sprayed the mouthful of liquid all on the floor.

The room was silenced as they watched the pale pink puddle as it spread.

"What is this,...Pepto Bismal?" Jasper caught himself before he cussed, but he spit into the barrel two more times, then examined the carton in his hand. It read strawberry milk.

"That's *it*." He glanced over to Chuckie who had acquired sausages from almost everyone at his table and was now demonstrating how he could wedge almost a dozen into his mouth at once. "Chuckie, Unky Jaspah is goin' *now*."

Jasper headed for the exit, in what was as close as he had gotten to a run in years. And, as the door closed, one tiny white mouse slipped its way to freedom right behind him.

A Revealing Memorial

The boys at the store were worried. Since the bridge over Colton Brook had washed out last fall, their annual Memorial Day tradition was in jeopardy. Jasper quickly stepped up and volunteered so that the holiday bouquet honoring those who had given service to their country could be tossed into the brook at the culvert down at his house. It seemed to him to be the patriotic thing to do.

He *did not*, however, tell Mother about the change in plans.

That Monday morning, she crouched behind the kitchen curtains as the entire enclave of the VFW, the Women's Auxiliary, all of the volunteer Fire

Department, Police Chief Ed Peterson, in full dress uniform, as well as a dozen Scouts and their parents, arrived in her front yard. Her mortification was amplified when Minister Smith from the Baptist Church led the entire entourage across the side yard, to the brook, passing directly under her clothesline.

There, on the line, in the side yard beside the brook, flapped Mother's complete wardrobe of sensible undergarments -brassieres, panties, slips and girdles (except for the set she was wearing, of course!) They were snapping their salute, proudly, in the spring breeze.

The remainder of the holiday was a most uncomfortable one for Jasper.

Arrested Development

"Jaspah?"

"Ayah"

"You bettah get down here to the station pretty quick." Jasper heard something desperate in police Chief Ed Peterson's voice. "I got your wife down here and she ain't happy. No. Not one bit."

"Mothuh? Did she get towed? Don't tell me that little tuna can of hers broke down. I told her to get it to the shop." Jasper babbled.

"Um, Jasper?" Ed interrupted. "I don't know exactly how to put this except plain. Uh, my wife's fool cousin, Tony, well, he was out on patrol this afternoon…" Ed was delaying the inevitable as long as he could. "Uh, Jaspah, he brought her in...*officially*. I need you to come down and get her out of here!"

Jasper heard a loudly familiar voice in the background, and then a crash.

"That idiot *arrested* her? What the hell happened, Ed?"

"Oh, she just kicked the trash barrel into the corner. She's pretty darn feisty just about now." offered Ed.

"No, no, I mean, what happened to make that pinhead even considered arresting her? Mothuh never does anythin' wrong! You know that, Ed!"

"It's too long to get into over the phone, Jaspah." There was another loud bang. "Leave that computer alone! You know how long it took us to get that in here! ... Jaspah, get down here now! " Ed called out and hung up.

Jasper grabbed his hat and ran out to his truck. Problem was, it wasn't in the yard. Mother's hatchback sat, shiny and clean, in the door yard. His truck was no where to be seen.

"Oh gawd, she took the truck. What was she thinkin'?"

Earlier that afternoon, Mother had headed over to the school to pick up her nephew Chuckie. It seemed that he had been asked to spend a little extra time after school with the vice principal. He had smuggled a few extra interesting items into class that morning. During snack time he had freed three very large frogs, a pocketful of worms (which he distributed with remarkable stealth, in various lunch boxes and milk cartons) and a handful of crickets. Chaos had reigned. The class had suffered the loss of three chocolate milks, a pudding cup, and entire bag of goldfish crackers. The crickets had chirred and popped about the room all day and had eventually infiltrated adjoining rooms. They, in their quest for freedom, had annihilated a computer hard drive, and had driven Mrs. Keefe, the music teacher, out of the building due to an anxiety attack related to her extreme fear of bugs.

When Vice Principal Cynthia Gordon heard about the invasion, she had requested that Chuckie come to her office after school so they could have a conversation about "appropriate behaviors at school and the consequences of his choices."

Chuckie wasn't all that sure what Ms. Gordon was talking about, but he found that if he nodded and said "Yes, Miz Gordon" enthusiastically, she would stop talking much sooner. He did enjoy the opportunity to visit the office and wave at all the parents, teachers and students who passed by after school. Even Uncle Jasper's pal, Cal Deckland came by.

Cal worked part time as a janitor each afternoon. Today, he and Chuckie had a game of pitch and toss. They wadded up sheets of paper from the recycling container and aimed at the vice principal's trash bin. Unfortunately, neither Cal nor Chuckie was a very good shot, so when Ms. Gordon returned to check on her student only to found her office snowed in under a paper ball blizzard. Cal quickly scooped up the scraps of paper and backed out of the office cheerfully. Parting, he and Chuckie slapped their ritual series of high, low and almost fives.

Ms. Gordon knew when she had lost the battle, and surrendered.

"Chuckie, I am going to call your Auntie to come get you now. You have spent enough time in detention. Can you just promise to leave the wildlife at home from now on?"

"Yes, Miz Gordon...but does that mean I can't be in de-tenting anymore? This was a lotso fun!"

In succession, Mother had received calls from the office, Chuckie's teacher, as well as a message containing an incoherent babble from Mrs. Keefe, the teacher who left school with cricket induced stress. She sensed the urgency to remove Chuckie from the building and raced out to her car. The engine of her compact car whined a bit, then rattled and coughed. Finally, all it could do was click. That was it. Concerned about her sweet little Chuckie waiting for her, she hurried into Jasper's truck.

The Dog had been riding daily with Jasper and

had left his mark clearly. The dash board and ceiling were covered with dirty paw prints; the seat was covered with old gnawed at, unrecognizable 'things.' She grabbed for the seat belt, forgetting that the straps had been chewed away by Jasper's canine pal. But, upon turning the key, the engine turned over confidently. Jasper was not necessarily neat or organized but he did take care of the working parts on that truck. He also was practical. He made most repairs whenever possible with duct tape, so much so that the once white truck now gleamed primarily silver. In fact he had just recently jury-rigged the muffler suspension with a creative assembly of duct tape, half of a wire hanger, an aluminum beer can and four of Mother's hair pins. It now hung snugly onto the back end… for the time being.

Mother traveled as fast as she dared. She was a stickler about staying within two miles per hour of the speed limit in any area. She had suffered her quota of honks, one fingered waves over the years, but she always kept to the law. The road was rutted like a mogul field. Cal was road agent but his budget was limited. He tried to keep the holes on one side of each road filled in, figuring that fixing half of all the roads was better than all of some. Unfortunately, it made for a wild and bumpy ride one way for everyone in town, and for Mother it was her…and the muffler's undoing.

The trucked bumped along, missing as many holes as Mother could negotiate. The steering on the old truck was not as tight as on her efficient little hatchback. With each kabump, a hairpin loosened and popped off the muffler. On the third turn on the Crooked Road, the beer can unfurled from the tail pipe and rolled out onto the road. Unfortunately, the can was intrinsic to Jasper's design and, also just as sadly, for Mother, it was about then that Tony Seneli, the chief's cousin-in-law and safety patrol officer, caught up with the truck and Mother.

The muffler and tail pipe dropped to the pavement, sending a shower of sparks out behind the vehicle. Scraping along, the now detached muffler repair, muffled nothing. Bellowing in protest, the truck continued to zig-zag across the road. Officer Seneli took his duty very seriously. As a part time officer, he only patrolled the street two evenings each week. Consequently, the only residents he knew were the kids who worked at the QuickCoffee drive through and the chief. He felt that his lack of familiarity with the townspeople was an asset and it heightened his ability to judge a criminal nature when he confronted one. He knew he was on to something big this time.

When Mother saw the blue flashing lights, she eased over to the side of the road to let him pass. To her surprise, the car pulled up behind her. So she came to a stop, her tires sinking into the loose sandy shoulder. She switched off the ignition, leaving the keys in place. (Jasper had warned her that he never took them out as the electrical connection "could be a real bear to rig up again.")

The young man wore his hat angled severely over his face. His uniform was crisp and sharply creased, unlike that of Chief Peterson, who had been known crumple into the same pants and shirt for several days in a row. The sunlight glinted off the numerous chrome plated attachments on the approaching officer which made Mother wonder how he could walk without jingling.

When he arrived at her door, she turned to smile at him.

"Well, hello, young man. What ever is the matter today?" she asked cheerfully.

Beneath the patent leather brim, the rest of his face was not smiling.

"Ma'am." The officer tipped his hat back slightly, peering at her through a pair of mirrored sunglasses which reflected her twin image. "Your license and registration, please, ma'am."

"Well, I could try to find it in here… Whatever would you need that for?" Mother heaved herself across the seat with a grunt. As she reached for the button on the glove compartment, she explained her need to leave. "You know, I am on the way to the school to pick up my young nephew. He will be waiting – he's only eight- just a little guy! So I really don't have much time to chat with you here."

Mother pushed the button on the compartment firmly, but it did not open.

"This truck is some temperamental. Are you sure you need that paper just now, son? " She inquired straightening up. "Is this some new check Ed started up? I am sure that he would have no problem with you letting me get over to the school without checking that paperwork just now. I bet I could have Jasper get you some donuts in the morning too if you like." She smiled sweetly at him.

"Ma'am? I cannot accept gratuities. Your license and registration?" He was not smiling. Mother leaned over again muttering to herself in confusion. She grabbed a large wrench from the floor and swung at the bottom of the glove box. The door fell off its hinge onto the floor followed by an assortment of fishing tackle, dead batteries, shot gun shells and several well chewed Dog "things."

"Oh, gawry day! It's in here somewhere. Hold on …" Mother sifted through the pile of junk now on the floor, and retrieved a coffee stained envelope. She shoved the soiled envelope out the window. "Here. Here it is. Phew, what a mess!"

She leaned back in the seat with a loud sigh.

"Ma'am?"

"What, dear? Can I leave now that you've checked that?"

"Your license too now." He still wasn't close to smiling.

Mother grabbed for her purse… but it wasn't in the truck. In her hurry to get her sweet little nephew, she had left it on the kitchen table.

"I don't have my license!" she blurted out.

"Ma'am? You are driving without a license?" Officer Seneli questioned.

"No, no, no! I have a license; I just don't have it now." Mother's frustration with the boy's inability to get to the point was starting to show. She checked her watch anxiously. "Officer … (reading his name tag) …*Senile*? I must get to school to get my…"

"Ma'am, am I to understand that you have lost your license?" he interrupted.

"Young man, I am sorry but rudeness is never acceptable. Please don't interrupt me when I am speaking. If Chief Peterson knew you were keeping me from getting Chuckie, I know he would not be happy with you. I think that I am going to have to speak to him about teaching you boys some manners!" she chastised.

"Right now, Ma'am." he said sarcastically. "I have a blurred, stained and torn registration for someone name Jasper, but no last name is readable. You have no license or identification and now   you're giving me an attitude? I had a notion to let you go before you got this attitude...but now, I'm going to have to run this registration,... if I can." He dangled the soiled scrap of paper from two fingers and returned to his cruiser, leaving Mother momentarily, in stunned silence. Then she began to mutter to herself.

"Attitude? Why how rude! He should know better... When I see Ed, he will hear about this. You'd think they would have better things to do out here rather than stopping law abiding townspeople... " She studied the man in her rear view mirror. Hat off in his vehicle, she could see a round hairless head. "Egghead! My Chuckie must be so worried about where his Auntie is. He probably thinks I forgot him. Oh my!" The panic began to build.

Officer Seneli returned.

"I cannot check your registration number has a third of it appears to have been gnawed off by something..."

"Oh what a Dog!" Mother exclaimed.

"What dog?" Seneli puzzled.

"The Dog...The Dog, of course!" Mother continued thinking of Jasper and his canine buddy "What a dang foolish imbecile! Doesn't know anything- No!" She turned to Officer Seneli and smiled smugly." Men can be such idiots!"

"What did you call me?" Officer Seneli drew himself up to his full height. His jaw hardened and he now seemed to have developed a twitch under his right eye. Then with a sly smile he said, " Lady, you just earned yourself a trip into town!"

"Now, you are doing the right thing! I am so glad you understand my predicament." Mother cried with joy "I do appreciate your consideration on this!"

Tony Seneli turned back toward his vehicle to let dispatch know he was bringing her in. Mother confidently started her engine; put the truck in gear. The rear wheel spun into the soft sand, kicking up a shower of dirt upon the creased and chromed policeman. Officer Seneli stood by his cruiser dumbfounded, momentarily frozen with disbelief.

Mother tore off into the village as fast as she dared. The tires squealed just a tad as she turned into the school driveway.

Tony Seneli pulled into the schoolyard just as Mother and Chuckie were leaving the school lobby. Vice Principal Gordon had pumped their hands vigorously and now had a hand on Chuckie's shoulder and Mother's arm, encouraging them both to be on their way. The cruiser peeled into the yard, blue lights flashing, siren wailing. It skidded to a halt, directly in front of the truck.

Tony Seneli leaped from the vehicle with a shout.

"NOBODY MOVE!" he pounced down in front of Mother, and hooked one bracelet of a pair of handcuffs onto her arm, locking them shut with a click. Mother opened her mouth to speak but nothing came out. He grabbed her other arm and clipped the other ring on her wrist.

"You are under arrest. You have a right to be silent, the right to an attorney – if you could find one crazy enough… And now you're coming in with me to the station!" He pulled her away to the cruiser. Chuckie and Cynthia Gordon stood slack jawed as the cruiser pulled away. Cynthia, started to cry as the blue lights disappeared, when she realized that she was still stuck with Chuckie.

Chief Ed Peterson was over at the store catching up on business, and snatching an afternoon coffee at the store with Neally Kendrick, head of the selectmen. He first heard his radio squawked when Tony called into dispatch indicating that he had a possible drunk driver in custody and was bringing her in. He noted that she had also been charged with fleeing the scene, resisting arrest and general misconduct.

"Wow, sounds like he's got a live one, there! Guess I better go help him out, Neally." Ed gulped the dregs of his coffee and hustled out the door. Ed was just about to climb into his vehicle when Tony's cruiser passed, blue light flashing and the siren wailing. He could see a woman with gray curls in the back seat, her head bounced and bobbed. As they passed, she turned to look out the window and Ed saw her face, contorted with rage, and even so, he knew it was Mother.

"Is that....? Oh, my gawd,...It is!" Ed launched from the lot and raced to town hall, screeching into the yard, and sprang out of the seat. He pounced on Tony, who had his hand on the door handle to just about to let the barracuda loose.

"HOLD IT! Tony, do not open that door... We gotta think this through! Oh, my Lord! Do you have any idea what you have done?"

"Sir? I'm gonna process this one. She's a real danger to the community, sir. Would you like to oversee the paperwork? I want to make sure I have it right. We certainly don't want this one getting away on a technicality!" Tony smiled proudly, and turned to unlock the door.

Mother eyed them through the window. She was slumped onto the door. With the last turn, she had tipped a bit, and with hands restrained, she had been unable to right herself. One shoulder and face were plastered to the window. Ed could hear her protesting but couldn't understand a word.

"Gawd, Tony, get her out of there! What were you thinking?"

"Okay, sir, if you're ready. Geez, I'm sure glad you showed up to back me up here. She seems real unpredictable! I had to apprehend her at the school,

Chief. She took off on me… tried to evade arrest. It was awesome!"

Mother had quieted some now but suddenly, she roared, pushing off the window with a tremendous heave. She turned her eyes on Tony, and, if looks could kill, Ed knew that boy would have been struck down there and then. He had never seen anyone look so murderous.

"Tony?"

"Yes, sir?"

"Get her out of the car. If looks could kill... you'd be a goner just now"

"Sir? She wants to kill me?"

"Now! Bring her inside, while I try to find Jasper." Ed sighed "And Tony, Get those cuffs off of her now." Ed turned on his heel and hoped he could find Jasper by phone.

Tony had gotten Mother out and on her feet again. He escorted her into the Town Hall, past Anne Marquis who was secretary to the selectmen and Cal Deckland who had raced over from the school as soon as he had heard from Emma what had happened.

"Hey, Seneli, what you gone and done here? You moron! Mothuh's never done anything wrong, ever!" Cal shouted at Tony.

The police officer ignored him. Tony was sure he had a dangerous prisoner and was determined to continue by the book. In the end, the Chief would thank him for it.

"Um, Tony, I'm not foolin' now. You really bettah let her go... I've *never* her seen her look so mad... Not even when The Dog dug up her grandma's rose bush..." warned Cal.

Mother walked in stony silence, reserving her steely glare for Officer Seneli. She marched proudly down the hall and into the office. Ed was on the phone, dialing. She turned to Tony.

"Take these handcuffs off me, right now, young man."

"Do it." directed Ed.

"Sir, are you sure? She's awful unpredictable..."

"*Do it* ... NOW!"

He unlocked the restraints, which dropped to the floor. As smoothly as any collegiate soccer star, Mother kicked the metal waste basket across the room with one of her sensibly clad feet.

"I have never in all the days I have lived in this town met such a *rude indiv*...Ed, when I get out of here I will be calling *your* wife..." and pointing at Tony, "and, *your mother*, Anthony, to let her know how *you* treat people. Hmm, bet that would make *her* day, eh? It would be best to know who you are dealin' with in this town!"

Ed again was surprised how such a sturdy woman could be so nimble. In a flash, Mother had her hands on the new laptop. She held it in one hand and opened the window with the other. She dangled the notebook out the window, Ed noted, just above the hood of Tony's cruiser parked below. He had to admit Mother, if anything, was observant and thorough.

"Put down the computer! Come on, we just got it - you know that!" Ed pleaded.

"Now, Ed, you know that I am a reasonable woman, but I,...I don't care any more. I'll have a *record* now! What difference will it make? You and this,..this..pinhead" she stumbled for the words. "Well, you've turned me into a desperate woman. I will drop it and Ed, you know me. I am a woman who is true to my word." She shot a venomous look at Tony, who was now hiding behind his only defense left, his mirror sunglasses. "Take those annoying things off your face-you look like a dang fool!"

"I got Jasper here on the line. What can we do to make this right? Please don't drop my new laptop! You don't want to hurt an innocent little computer! What do you really want?"

"You bring my little Chuckie to me from school and I'll give you back your computer. I want to take him home. That poor little fellow must be worried sick about where I am," she turned, snarling like a rabid fisher cat. "But keep Officer Denali over there out of my way."

"Seneli... go get Chuckie, Code 3."

"Code 3, Chief?" Tony questioned. "I dunno... are you sure?"

"CODE 3! This is an emergency. Get that kid and get back here."

"Oh yes...and make sure Chuckie buckles up, will you?" Mother reminded him sweetly.

Epilogue:

Officer Tony Seneli did as he was told. Chuckie had a thrilling ride in the police car. Jasper skidded into town, having revived Mother's compact car, and driving it faster than it had ever been driven in the twelve years that they had owned it. Ed, in fact did save the computer, but had to declare the dented trash barrel a complete loss. He dropped all charges against Mother, declaring that the whole event a vast misunderstanding.

Tony Seneli is now working security at dollar store near Concord, having been reprimanded by his mother, who did get an earful in a phone call from Mother. Ed's wife told him that her nephew had out grown his welcome in his department, and he had hired Cal Deckland's brother, Jake, who had grown up in town and knew everyone.

Mother did recover from the unfortunate encounter, but Jasper still fears to mention it,   as somehow it all became his fault when they arrived home. He wasn't sure how that happened but Mother sputtered on about his complicity for hours. Knowing that there was no way to change her mind, he just took the barrage, nodding and joining with an occasional "Ayuh, of course, Mothuh!" He knew what she needed and was there for her, as always, in the end.

The Embarrassment

Typically, breakfast for Jasper was a fairly unpretentious event. There was always coffee, steamy and black, never with any abominable additives. Jasper was a shredded wheat man by routine. Two big biscuits from a wax paper stack with whole milk, kept him regular and happy. Muesli was something Gawmer might mix to feed his pigs and once, in his youth, Jasper had felt adventurous and added some sliced banana to his bowl. But that had been a mistake. Nope. Jasper kept it simple and that kept Jasper happy.

Mother, over the years, had tried to tempt him with a bit of variety. She had tried to sprinkle some blueberries on sugar frosted wheat bits. She had tried a plate of colorful melon chunks from the farm stand right down the road. She had even tried French toast made with eggs from their own chickens. Jasper would have none of it.

"My usual keeps me just fine. Regularity is somethin' a man values as he ages."

Mother wondered what she had been thinking when she had signed them up to attend her church Guild trip to the regionally famous Luncheon Bruncheon in Concord. They would be traveling on a lovely air conditioned motor coach after Sunday Mass. The brunch was presented in the courtyard garden room of the High-Hat Wander Inn. Mother in desperation had signed them up for the trip. She hated that she had needed to compete with Emma VanShuke, who's trim, handsome husband happily attended all of the church functions and even danced without being begged or bribed. She had done it. Mother had picked up the pen on the table at the back of the church and had written their names in on line 25 and 26 of the sign up sheet, in front of Father McDonald and everyone.

Emma, who was on the organizing committee, peered at Mother through the tops of her designer bifocals.

"Dear, are you sure that you want two tickets? You of all people must know how Jasper can be at times. I mean no offense of course, dear, but shouldn't you ask him if he can *behave*, um, I mean,… if he will *attend* before you sign up?"

The silence in the room would have made Jesus proud at a Good Friday service, but for Sunday morning, it was nothing but stony cold.

Mother felt the eyes burning down on her, looks of sympathy from some and others filled will cool anticipation of another juicy tidbit to discuss before Rosary on Tuesday night. She swallowed hard and forced a light chuckle, remarking loudly so all might hear.

"Oh Emma, if course Jasper will love it! He's just a little shy. You don't know him as well as you think. He's really just a big old teddy bear!" With that, Mother turned tail for the parking lot as quickly as her sensible shoes would take her.

Three weeks later, after much cajoling and sweet talk, Jasper still refused to go along. Finally, Mother played her trump card! It was Saturday night before the big Bruncheon excursion.

'Well, you don't go Jasper, I'll tell you what, you can just forget about your regular Saturday evening 'special', if you catch my meaning, Mister–man?" As if to punctuate her meaning, the bathroom door slammed shut and the door was locked. Jasper heard the water running for what he expected would be a marathon tub, candle and romance novel session for

Mother. That meant he would be spending his Saturday alone.

"JAY-sus" He muttered with resignation, removing his plaid dress shirt and his best green work pants from the closet. "JAY-sus hangin' on a cross...."

"Jaspah!!!"

"Okay, I'll go, Mother." he sighed submissively.

The deal was sealed. Jasper was going to be on that bus. Mother shut off the tap and wafted into the room through a veil of steam.

"You'll see, honey! It'll be so much fun!" She beckoned to him with a victorious wink and a wiggle.

Jasper was ready bright and early, but spent his holy hour as he did most mornings, holding court at the Village store coffee pot. He figured that if he kept a regular schedule, God Almighty would know exactly where to find him on any given day.

He was the first on the motor coach and took a seat right behind the driver, so he could make sure they took the most direct route. He knew a few short cuts which he was sure would be unfamiliar to the driver. Mother didn't care. She actually enjoyed sitting up front, greeting all the ladies of the rosary group with a slightly smug smile for each. En route, she deluded herself with a fantasy that she had been playing in her head for the last week. She had heard once on Oprah that it was beneficial to visualize the result you wanted.

In her ideal world, she and Jasper were nibbling the delectable morsels across a crisp linen tablecloth. There were white china plates, gleaming silverware and crystal goblets of icy water sparkling beneath the twinkling of a thousand miniature lights from a real chandelier. She and he would chat amiably with her friends from church and they would enjoy every moment.

What *had* she been thinking?

The bus rolled up to the Wander Inn, where it spit them into the lobby of the hotel.

"Church of the Holy Rosary? Ladies? Your group should follow me this way." The suited man led them past the three buffet tables loaded with food. The smell was heavenly. Mother could have sworn that she heard growls from several of the group. Most of them hadn't eaten since the previous night, holding with the old church tradition of fasting. It had actually become a competitive event for some of the more faithful to see who could be the most penitent. Miss Abigail Thoroughgood almost fainted as she passed the buffet, and had to be helped away by her sister, Annie.

Jasper started grumbling when they hit the lobby. He was not loud enough for any one to understand his words, except for Mother, of course who knew his language. All they could get was the steady rumbling from deep in his throat and an occasional "gawdammit." or "stupid pinhead". Mother tried coughing and commenting on the lovely décor as a distraction. She almost believed it would work.

Jasper sat with a loud harrumph, taking the big chair at the head of the table; the seat clearly had been reserved for Father McDonald. Several people cleared their throats to get his attention. Mother quickly whispered in his ear. But once settled, Jasper was not to be moved.

"Mothuh, that skinny boned preacher doesn't need a big chair like this. This one is built for a working fella like me. Besides, isn't he a man of his people an' all that stuff?"

Mercifully, Father McDonald announced from behind a seat in the middle of the long table, that he would now offer the blessing. Mother yanked on Jasper's collar till he choked a bit, which forced him to rise slightly from his chair to relieve the pressure on his throat.

Father went on for a bit, praising the bounty which they had been given (and paid for, as Jasper saw it.) Eventually the man finished but not before Jasper interrupted.

"Hey, how about amen? You know, Father, Son, Amen?"

The praying over, Mother released her grasp on her husband and waited momentarily in hopes that

Jasper would remember some elemental manners and hold out the chair for her but it did not surprise her to see that he was already headed for the buffet. She perched on her seat and shook out the cloth napkin and sipped a bit of water.

Although Jasper was ready to begin, the restaurant staff was still reloading the buffet table for their large group and he was forced to hold off his assault on the mounds of food. Eventually, the hostess waved him on, tired of his hovering and loud commentary. In a flash, Jasper had filled a large plate and as he headed back to his seat, he called across the room to Mother.

"Psssst! Watch out for that casserole stuff. It's some sort of gluck with eggs and some green stuff… I was smart. I grabbed a taste before I put it on the plate! It's the worse thin' I've tasted since I tried that salt lick you put out in the yard for the deer!" Jasper breezed on over to his seat and began inhaling food from the mound on his plate.

It was like a bad accident from which the Guild ladies couldn't look away, Mother included. Most of the group stared in amazement, the food on their own plates growing cold, their forks balanced in their fingers without ambition. They could not even detect if he was chewing, rather he appeared to be washing it all back with large swigs of coffee from the advertised "never-ending mug".

Mother excused herself quietly and retreated to the back side of the buffet. She took a small portion of a few dishes, leaving plenty of room for a few sweets from the dessert buffet later. When she returned to the table, she found Jasper wiping his now empty plate clean with a crust of bread.

"Ya know, dear, this brunch-on thing ain't so bad. I am glad that I had my shredded wheat early on, so now this buffett isn't gonna upset my innards. I believe I am going to get some of that roasted beef that they are carving over there! "With that, he pushed aside his plate and headed up to the buffet once again. He returned shortly toting an large, oval tray heaped with slices of rare beef, potatoes and cinnamon buns.

"Look-at what I found, Mothuh! They were hiding the big plates under the tomatoes and cukes … I just scooped them into the salad bowl and I found me a real man size plate." Mother sighed quietly, shaded a bit more red with embarrassment, and continued to nibble her food.

Fortunately, Jasper's preoccupation with his feed kept him from involving himself in much of the conversation at the table. At one point during his third pass through the buffet he did take exception when Rob Roundtree took the last four pieces of the bacon in the pan and had shouted.

"Hey, Roundtree! Leave a few pork rinds for the rest of us back here. Your pants are already pretty snug in the be-hind, fella!"

By 2:30, when Father McDonald asked them all to bow their heads in a prayer of thanksgiving, Jasper had stacked six dirty plates in front of him, including the buffet platter and was swiping a seventh.

"Now that was perty darn tasty! I believe I'm done." Jasper leaned back in his seat and belched with satisfaction.

"JASP-ah!" hissed mother. Losing her temper, she aimed a well placed kick to his shin. "Enough now.... DAMMIT ...*You are an embarrassment*!"

Suddenly, Mother realized that she was no longer whispering. The entire Ladies Guild and Father McDonald had just noted that her curse had been perfectly timed with the end of Father's prayer so they heard distinctly, as if with one voice;

"Thank you, Oh Lord, our God...." "DAMMIT! *You are an embarrassment!"*

The ride home was silent, except for steady and even snoring and an occasional belch from Jasper as he contentedly digested his food. As for Mother, she just stewed, regretting mightily the one time she had pried Jasper from his 'regularity.'

Weigh, the People

Mother had been going to Doctor Jeremiah Calef for years. She maintained her trim yet substantial figure proudly. It was not without effort. She ate a balanced diet, and exercised daily. Jasper was no help. Other couples might enjoy sharing an evening meal of salad, or they might take a stroll together down a peaceful country road. Jasper would have none of that. He maintained his skinny behind on a diet of donuts, hot dogs and coffee with extra cream and sugar. Doc Calef said Jasper's perfect health was an anomaly of modern medicine.

Mother checked her weight on an old but reliable floor scale each Monday morning. It was solid metal and she had always trusted its measure. This regularity kept her honest at pot luck suppers and at coffee hour after church each Sunday.

This morning, Miriam Standish, Doc Calef's nurse, checked Mother in for her annual physical, babbling incessantly, as she always did, when Mother, tactfully redirected her.

"So, Miriam, do you have a new scale here?.... My, isn't it fancy!"

"Oh yes! This is state of the art. Doc had to replace the old one last month. He let Old Man Gawmer weigh his prize sugar pumpkin for the fair. I don't know what he was thinking! That pumpkin was sizeable and well, the old scale got.... squashed!" Miriam laughed and nudged Mother. "Isn't that so funny? We've been doing that joke ever since."

"Oh, for heaven's sake, Miriam, Why did he let Gawmer weigh his pumpkin on the office scale?"

"Well, dear, it seems that Doc was planning to put a few dollars on it in the Pumpkin Pool at the fair. Doesn't Jasper put something down on one? Well, Doc isn't much of a risk taker and he figured they better check on Gawmer's entry so he wouldn't be taken for too many dollars. "

"Isn't that cheating?" asked Mother.

"I think so, but he doesn't see it that way." Miriam paused to for a gulp of air. "Anyway, that pumpkin was just too much for the 'Old Beast.'   Did you know that's what I used to call that scale? It was pretty ugly but you could count on it, you know. It was reliable. Now, this monstrosity is totally different. Doc has to have a technician from the company come out here to check it every month. Everything is so complicated these days, isn't it?"

Mother just nodded, unable to wedge a syllable in politely.

"Now why don't you hop up there and we'll see what it says to us." Miriam encouraged. She pressed a green button on the display panel, it beeped and a window on the front of the scale lit up.

Confidently, Mother removed her sensible (and rather weighty) shoes and stepped onto the gleaming stainless steel platform with confidence. Despite her friendship and long term association with Miriam, Mother did not "hop" anywhere. The numbers blinked then the machine counted down audibly, as if ready for blast off.

"Ohh, it talks?" exclaimed Mother.

With authority an electronic voice declared, "One-hundred-seventy-seven."

Miriam propped her clipboard on her ample chest and copied the number onto Mother's chart.

"Well, dear you did gain a bit this year but I suppose that's to be expected at your age. It's alright; they say that metabolism kicks back on later. Okay, you can hop down now."

"One hundred and *seventy*-seven pounds?"

Mother sputtered like and old outboard motor trying to catch after a long winter.

"*One hundred and seventy-seven*?" she yelped. She did not step down and instead, she gave the stand a hard kick. She stamped her sizable yet still unclad feet on the shiny steel platform. "I have never been, nor am I now, been one hundred and seventy *anything*! Miriam Standish, I insist that you erase that number now, and do it over, thank you very much. This scale is wrong."

Mother folder her arms and refused to move.

"Now, dear," Miriam cooed. "It's alright. This number is a little bit different, but Doc says I have to use this number now. He knows that it will even out over time. Come on now, dear, hop down now."

"Miriam, I refuse to accept this. You do not have my permission to use this number, do you hear me? You can tell Doc and his technician friend that they are sadly mistaken. You can also tell him that this is the last time I evah step up on that nasty thing willingly."

"You can tell him yourself," Miriam sighed, "but first I need to take your blood pressure dear."

Mother rolled her eyes, realizing that now yet another measurement would be exaggerated as well.

Doc was as flexible as an iron skillet. Mother had pleaded her case, to the point that he had asked whether she might need a prescription for an anti-anxiety medicine.

After driving away from the office, the whole incident still rankled her. That scale was obviously dysfunctional. It was simply wrong. Someone needed to step up and help the community. She had always been one to do what was right. She stopped over to the store for a cup of coffee, a clove of garlic and Squeezy Lemon to make a marinade later. Back in the car, she intended to turn back down the road to home, but instead angled back across the way to Doc's office. She planned to re-open the weight debate with Doc. That machine was wrong and he had to see it. And, she would also get the company name and as a responsible consumer, contact the manufacturer of the poorly engineered product

"Miriam? You here?" Mother had entered the waiting area and saw no one. From the back room she heard Doc Calef snoring loudly. Everyone in town knew Doc "checked his paperwork" in back during the noon hour. "Miriam?"

No one answered. Not a soul had seen her enter. She opened the half door between the waiting room and the office and tiptoed over to the scale.

"Now you,....*You* are an evil machine, you know that don't you?" She stared it down considering its chrome highlights. She ran her hand across the display panel "Well, you may be pretty but you're wrong, you know! I am not an ounce over 152! Oh my! Now who's crazy? I am arguing with a machine!"

Mother spied a manufacturer label on the stand and leaned forward to read the contact information so she could write a letter of complaint to the manufacturer. She rested her coffee hand on the display to help her balance. As she leaned, the machine turned on with a piercing *beep*. Startled, she squeezed the foam cup of coffee and the contents Niagrah-ed all over the display.

"Oh, my! Oh, dear!" Mother grabbed at her pockets for her inevitable stash of linty tissues and came forth with only the Squeezy Lemon which she had pocketed so as not to have to waste a bag at the store. She left the lemon on the scale and ran across the office to grab a box of tissues.

She returned to the scale in time to see that the lemon was open and the liquid was now mixed with the coffee and trickling into the scale's electronic panel. As she dabbed at the machine with tissues, she stumbled onto the platform and the electronic troll inside began to countdown.

"Onnne, two, th-thh –thhrreeeeeee-iiiiiee."

Mother thought she heard a slight gurgle and then a quiet fizzt. The screen blinked once, then twice, and then the numbers on the display became a series of gray and black geometric shapes. Finally from deep within the support post, came a high pitched whine, then at last, all went quiet and dark. Mother gave the scale a nudge with her foot, then backed away.

"Oh my," Mother patted the now silent machine dry. She put the now empty Squeezy Lemon back in her pocket along with the crumpled tissues and pressed the reset button on the display. Nothing. She picked up the crumpled cup and pressed "On." Nothing. Taking a pen and a sticky note from Miriam's desk, she scribbled a note:

"Dear Miriam, I am sorry but there was an accident. I will be back later when Doc is done with his 'paperwork.'"

She pasted the note on the scale and marched out to her car. As the door slammed behind her the note's sticky unstuck and it fluttered to floor under the medical supply cabinet.

On her way home, Mother passed the church and felt she needed to own up to her responsibility in the killing of the innocent machinery, accidental or not. It was the first time she had ever destroyed something... and she hated to admit that it felt pretty good. Vanquishing an enemy, even by accident, was wrong but the results somehow seemed right. Father MacDonald was in the confessional just finishing up with old Maisey Dobbins who stopped in to say her confession every day at lunch time just in case she passed away that night. Mother entered the confessional kneeled and got directly to the point.

"Bless me Father for I have sinned, sort of. You know I was just here last weekend, but, well, something just came up." She told Father her whole story and he listened patiently. When she was done he addressed her kindly.

"Now, this was an accident and, of course, it was wrong to ruin that machine, but you didn't do it on purpose."

"But I did do it and…actually felt glad after. Isn't that sinful, Father?" she interrupted.

"Well, not technically. Personally, you did me a favor! I hope that Doc doesn't replace that thing. I nearly had a heart attack when I weighed in on it last week." Father MacDonald sighed loudly and paused. He ruffled his sparse hair with his fingers and he turned toward Mother. "Why don't you say ten Our Fathers for a penance, if it'll make you feel better, but I see this as a true act of God. I mean that thing was not really doing the town any good, at all."

One thing Mother always loved about her Jasper was his ability to simplify even the most complicated situation. She drove home, made a bowl of soup and when Jasper got in, told him the whole story. He listened and then was quiet for a moment.

"Mothuh, hold on here just a minute or two. I gotta go out to the barn." And he vanished out the door. Mother wasn't sure what to think but she had learned long ago that waiting on Jasper was part of the bargain of being married to such a unique man. So she waited.

Within the hour, Jasper returned.

"Come on outside for a minute. I think I got the answer to your problems, Mothuh" He escorted her into the yard and there in the back of his rusty old truck was Doc's old scale.

"But, Jaspah, that scale was broken!... Gawmer's pumpkin,...the Fair...How did you get it here?" Mother stammered in disbelief.

"Mothuh, you know me better than that. Doc, that old fool... threw this scale into the metal pile at the transfer station. Me and Cal pulled it out as soon as he left. I figured that this year I was gonna win the Pumpkin Pool and he would never know what happened. I brought it home and fixed that sprung spring underneath and she's good as new. I'll go bring it back to Doc so he can turn in that thing that upset you so and use something more reliable." He turned back to Mother but she wasn't listening. She had climbed up into the truck bed and was standing, barefoot, on the scale.

"Just as I said..." confirmed Mother, sliding the weights into place. "One hundred and fifty- two."

Booking it for Freedom

"I'm sorry, dear, but you need to have your library card to take out books." Librarian Ellie Mercer reached for the small stack of books Mother had placed on the check out desk. Ellie slid them toward her guarding them authoritatively

"I don't think I have my card here, Ellie." Mother slung her rather substantial purse up onto the desk with thud and rummaged through it. "Can't I just take that little pile today and next time I'll bring the card around? You know my number."

"The card is now required."

"But, Ellie, I have been coming here now for years! Jasper went to school with your Benny. Can't you just trust me and let it go just this once?"

"Now I could but how would I explain that to another patron who gets wind of it and wants to know why I can't let it go for them too!" Ellie sighed. "Nope, I do understand your disappointment, dear, but the state library conference recommended this for our country's security."

"What?"

"Well, you see, dear, we librarians are on the front lines of homeland security. We need to reduce the possibility that information could get into the wrong hands." Ellie glanced around the area and whispered, "You know,... *terrorists*!"

"Well, you and I both know that I am *not* a terrorist, Ellie. I can't find that card in here!" Mother sighed. "Can't you just let me have those today?"

"That just wouldn't be fair. Besides, that's not the point. If I let you have these books without your card then this library would be a weak link in the chain of our country's security...What if terrorists found out and came *here*?" Ellie clutched the books to her ample bosom. "We are all connected and if I give in to you, well who knows where it might lead?"

"Ellie! All I have is a couple of romance novels and a book on composting for Jaspah. He's determined to make a better manure mixture than Melanie. How in Heaven's name will that compromise our country's security?" cried Mother. She tried tact. "I have to watch my nephew, Chuckie in just a little while. Maybe I could take the books and I'll have Martha run by here with my card when she goes out? How would that be?"

"Well, you know I haven't seen Martha in an age! Is she working up at the toll booth again?" As Mother hoped, Ellie relaxed her grip, as she had always needed at least one hand to talk. Mother had excellent reflexes, so as Ellie lifted one hand to point north at the toll booth, she pounced on the paperbacks as quickly as a cat.

"Let go." commanded Ellie who held on one handed and deftly reclaimed her territory with the other in the cross clutch.

"Oh, Ellie, please?" Mother pleaded

"I am just doing my part." said Ellie, winning the battle, strengthened by her patriotism. She slid the books into her desk drawer, turned the key in the lock and dropped it down the front of her blouse into the depths of that ample bosom. "I'll put these books on reserve for three days. You go home and when you find your card, you can come back and check them out."

Mother heaved her purse onto her shoulder and turned to go when she heard Ellie mutter. "I'm meaning that compost book alone has a trove of chemical information in... Maybe Jasper is thinking of making some sort of methane-manure explosive!"

"A manure bomb? Oh, Ellie now you have completely lost it. Everyone in town knows the only thing explosive about Jaspah is when he finishes a plate of beans! I guess I'll come back later when you have regained your senses." Mother headed out the door with a firm steady step, in her sensible shoes.

It was then that Ellie heard a rustling in the back corner of the large room. Old Man Gawmer appeared, hesitating at the end of the large book shelf. In his hand he held a book titled "Radio Monitored Animal Husbandry."

"Well, I suppose you ain't a gonna let me take a loaner on this one, and I sure ain't gonna fight ya for it." he shrugged, tucking the volume back in the stack, and hustled out the door behind Mother.

Political Transfer

Jasper answered the phone and was caught by yet another primary election survey.

"Gawry! You would think that those fools would have better things they could think of to do with their money?" Jasper sighed with disgust. "But, I bet you didn't realize that we have had made a difference to elections in the past. Them polly-tishans better pay attention because comin' here can make or break 'em!

"Well, sir, I just have a few questions for you, so it should be fairly quick!" replied the young female voice on the other end of the connection.

"I suppose you think so, don't you? Well tell you what, let me just tell you a little story about a time not so long ago when we had a special visitor and had the chance to turn the tide of his-story!"

With that, Jasper started and the caller was stuck. "It happened like this…."

Cal Deckland was a regular fellow, easy going and good natured. Jasper had known him since high school and they had been meeting at the store for coffee each morning since. The men vehemently denied that they ever gossiped. No, they discussed current events. They "opinionated" about the political scene. They knew that they had important ideas and would, if given the voice and the opportunity, make a critical difference in their world.

"Jaspah, you know what I been thinkin'?" Cal offered as he sucked in a mouthful of coffee.

"Whaaa….?" Jasper regarded Cal seriously across the wheel of a giant cinnamon roll.

"I think that if we made them candidates work down at the transfer station for just one day, they would have a whole different perspective on how real Americans live." He interrupted himself briefly with a belch. "You know all sorts of people come through the facility on any given day and you can tell a lot about 'em just by lookin' at their trash."

"Ayuh." Jasper continued to unravel the gooey spiral, chewing on it with conviction. "I suppose if any of them poli-tee-cal types did an honest day's work, they'd stop yap-yap-yipping and start listening to fellas like us who really know what's goin' on!"

"You know what I'm gonna do, Jaspah? I'm gonna invite them ovah to the facility. I bet they don't have the man-parts to show up … But I'm gonna do it anyway! Hey Neally, whatcha think? That'd be okay with the town right?"

Neally Kendrick, head of the town select board, sat hidden behind the latest issue of Field and Stream, which he had filched from the magazine rack behind him. He ruffled the pages and added an indefinite "Hmm? Ah yah…sure."

…Which Jaspah and Cal took to be a complete and official endorsement of the plan.

A few coffees later, Jasper and Cal were bumping along the Turnpike Road in the truck on the way to the transfer station.

"You gonna invite them all, Cal, or just those Jackasses?" Jasper asked.

"I dunno if that's advisable, Jasper." Cal answered."I mean, I want to be fair and ask all of them, not just the ones who are jerks!"

"Don't be a pinhead! I meant Jackasses… like donkeys? The Republicans are fatties, or some people call 'em elephants and those Dem-oh-cats are donkeys or jackasses. You know, I never had much use for politicians anyway. Don't tell him, but even Neally is pretty useless most of the time. They never listen, and they always say they're gonna do stuff and then they don't. You can ask them to come, but it won't make one bit of difference about what they'll do in the end" Cal hopped down from the truck to unlock the gate, and Jasper slumped into his seat, entirely spent by his speech.

Back in the truck, Cal nodded and shifted into drive with determination.

"Nope, I'm gonna invite all of them. It's only fair."

When they had opened up the office, Cal slid a clean piece of paper into the old Smith Corona perched on the corner of his desk. "I'll even offer to buy 'em a coffee at the store if they'll come." He pecked at the keys with confidence.

"Ayuh. Good idea." agreed Jasper.

"You know, it's all about the trash. They could learn so much when they see how people deal with their trash! I mean it's the great equalizer. Everybody makes trash. Everyone has to take it somewhere to throw it out- well except maybe the rich ones. They actually make more garbage, but they just pay someone else to pitch it for 'em."

"Ayuh, you know I agree, Cal. Heck I work here too. I've seen it all, for myself. That Joe Garner practically gift wraps his garbage. He was one of those engineers before he retired. His bags are always exactly the same size, and he binds them up with string."

"I know, I know!" Cal nodded. "Then there's that Dog Lady up on County Road. She brings in her truck loaded with sparkling clean dog food cans every two weeks. I can't figure out if she hand washes them or loads up her dishwasher with 'em. How many dogs she got anyway?"

"Dunno...I've seen four or five big ones up there.. but they're always running around so they're dang hard to count!" Jasper whacked at a stained Mr. Coffee to start up a fresh pot.

Cal focused on his typing, which took most of the rest of the morning. Jasper worked diligently for almost an hour, checking the bins, and sweeping up the office. Each time a car backed up to the bin, he went out to check out their load. Much to Mother's dismay, most of Jasper's selflessness about helping his pal Cal at the dump, was really an excuse to get first pick of the 'good' stuff. Jasper was a dumpie. He always found something special, and each item was veritable treasure. Mother and Jasper's barn was full of "treasure" with tinkering potential.

Mrs. McGuire drove in with an electric back massager pad that she said had been working but occasionally gave her a "doozy of a jolt". Jasper agreed with her and helped her bring it into the shed.

As soon as she had pulled away with a cheery wave, Jasper scooped up the pad, bringing it up to the office.

"Cal, look at this massaginator thing! I can fix it up for Mothuh. She'll love it."

Cal's office itself was an eclectic mix of styles gleaned from the leavings of friends and neighbors.

They had set up a bamboo bar complete with three zebra-striped, padded stools. They had added a genuine plastic crystal vase, which held a few blue silk dahlias. Glowing, behind the bar, stood a bronze naked goddess floor lamp. Staring down from the wall was a genuine oil painting on velvet of a big-eyed bull dog playing poker. They were proud of their ability to skim the best of the town's trash before it hit the dumpsters.

Cal finished the letters and helped Jasper finish up their chores, and put up the lunch sign, which read "Leave your trash, but don't leave a MESS!" and then headed down the Turnpike road into town for lunch. The dump remained open during lunch on the honor system. Cal believed the friendly sign set a tone of honesty at the facility, and it was respected by the townspeople.

When the boys arrived at the store, they leaped from the rusty truck, excited to see that Nacky Sweinworth was at the register by the window. Normally, this sight would have been reason enough to take another trip around the lake to avoid her. Nacky was the local representative for the Coalition of Free

Thinkers, who decreed that they were the true Yankees. They prided themselves on saying exactly what they thought. Jasper had always managed to do the same but never felt the need to join a club for it. Cal and Jasper knew that Nacky had the political connections that they needed, and they lighted down on her like black flies on a sweaty fisherman.

"Why Nacky, ain't you looking fine today! Let us help you with your bags," Jasper extended a greasy hand to grab her groceries. She slapped at his hand and screeched, as only a Free Thinker could.

"Jaspah! Get your grubby mitts off my food! You and Deckland reek of garbage!" She tried to edge by Cal, her nose turned up and away from the pair.

"Come on, Nacky, we need your help. You know all the politicians in the state and all the candy-dates and we need to make a connection." Cal waved several envelopes, each smudged with his dirty fingerprints. "We need the real addresses for some of those polly-tishans. I know you know 'em all. You probably have your address book right in there!"

He poked at her purse which she clutched like a receiver on a last desperate try for the winning touchdown. She even held her right arm up in a defensive position across her ample chest.

Then she saw the name on one of the envelopes and snatched it from Cal's grip.

"'*Hillary Clinton*'?" she squealed. "What in all that is holy would entice you two to write to Ms. Clinton? I don't even dare to imagine what this says, although, I suppose that even you two are entitled to freedom of speech. Now, back off a bit and explain what you want here"

Jasper cleared his throat and stepped back. He grabbed at Cal's shirt and dragged him back a foot.

"We need addresses. We're sending this letter to her, and some others, airing our concerns about trash and recyclin' and such. Nacky, you an' I both know that's a major thing for them poli-tishans and you know where they take their mail. So how 'bout it?"

Nacky still clutched her purse protectively, but she loosened her grip so that she could snap the soiled envelope from Cal's fingers.

"Well, I'll tell you what. I will address this letter for you, and the Free Thinkers will spring for the stamp! The rest there, you'll have to look up at the library." she declared.

"Um, okay, that's a deal," Cal agreed tentatively. "You promise you'll mail that one today?"

"Of course I will, boys. You can trust the word of a Free Thinker!" She quickly made her escape, waving at them cheerfully from her car as she backed out of the lot.

"You think we should follow her?" Jasper offered.

"Naw. She'll do it. Besides, I'll just call Bobby Sullivan down to the post office. He'll let me know if she drops it off."

"Well anothuh good idea launched, eh Cal? How about I buy you a couple of steamed dogs for lunch?" Jasper licked his lips with anticipation.

Later that afternoon, Bobby did confirm that the letter had gone out with the afternoon bag to the city post office. Cal went back to the dump to work, and Jasper returned home to work on fixing up the "massaginator" for Mother.

They didn't think about it much over the next few weeks as springtime was notoriously a busy season at the dump. Townsfolk cleaned, sorted and pitched their extra stuff as soon as the thaw started. Cal had Jasper volunteering full time to keep the place clean and organized. Cal was wrapped up with inventory and keeping the recycling hoppers compacted. He prided himself on being able to stuff more of anything into a packer trailer than any other member of the Society of Transfer Union Facilities, Ecology and Recycling (S.T.U.F.E.R.) He had long been admired by other members for his stuffing skills.

Cal was struggling to compact some metal straps that Joe Garner had dropped into the metal bin, left over from one of his inventions. The fifteen foot long strips were springy and flexible, and kept snaking around in the bin so that the compacter head couldn't get a grip on them. He shoved the pole down in the bin one last time to "persuade" the material into submission, when Bobby skidded up the drive in his ancient mail jeep..

"CAL! JASPAH! Get out here quick! You got an answer!" He waved a large white envelope emblazoned with a border of little red, white, and blue flags. "Hurry, you knob-heads."

Cal took his hand off the lever, and the strips of metal sprang out of the hopper like a giant can of magic snakes.

"Bobby, what are you hollerin' about? Jeez-um, the way you came in here, you'd think the town hall was on fire! It ain't, is it?" Cal hurdled the coils of steel, and sprang to a spot next to Bobby.
"What the heck is the matter?"

"You got a letter here, Cal!" Bobby paused to catch his breath. "I think it's from Hillary Clinton herself"

Cal snatched the envelope from his hand and tore at it.

"Oh, my gawd! ....Jaspah! Get over here!"

Jasper never hurried anywhere, but he increased his normal speed from snail to tortoise, given the urgency in Cal's voice.

"What are you yappin' about Cal? Jeez, I almost had all those National Ge-oh-graphics sorted out in the swap shop. Now I have to come out here before I was done and they all slid down all over the place."

"Quit your griping. Look-it, Jasper, it's an official letter from Hillary Clinton!" He ripped at the envelope and unfolded the flag burdened stationary.

" '*Dear Mr. Duckland, I am happy to hear from concerned citizens....*' She's got my name all wrong...," Cal trailed off as he skimmed the letter, reading it to himself.

"So what's it say? Is she coming to the dump?" Jasper bounced up and down in front of Cal. Bobby stood behind him trying to read the letter over his shoulder.

"Here it is!...'*Public employees are the back bone of our infrastructure, and I think is critical that the American people extend their hand and enter into a conversation with you about recycling and the future of our planet*'.. Hey, perty cool, eh, Jaspah? We know we're important but she thinks we're important too, eh?" Cal smiled with satisfaction. "Here it is, at the bottom. '*We will plan to add you to our campaign tour on March 28. Our security team will be contacting you.*' That's only three days from now!"

Jasper looked at his watch and then glanced around the station at the piles of tires, the mulch to be mixed, and magazines to be stacked.

"Well, we better get crackin'! We gotta clean up and work up some projects for her to help out with."

121

"Ayuh!" Cal turned back to his hopper and compacted with renewed vigor.

The campaign manager did contact town hall to request a police escort for Senator Clinton's entourage. Chief Ed Peterson confirmed the coverage, especially since Cal had promised to spring for coffee that day. He would have a car available as an escort, and one other cruiser would be at the four corners in the center of town, ready to hold back the traffic. Security would be a priority.

Cal and Jasper refused all offers for an official reception. Mother volunteered to bring a loaf of her famous zucchini-pumpkin-chocolate-chip-nut-bread, and the boys felt that would be plenty for everyone. She also planned to bring up a jug of grape Zarex, and of course, there would be coffee. The boys were adamant that Mrs. Clinton had accepted their invitation to learn about trash, and they did not intend to have a lot of time to chat over coffee and cake. This was to be a hands-on learning experience for the senator.

The big day dawned and the raw damp air foretold of nasty weather. Heavy rain was expected and with mud season was fully under way, the Turnpike Road was now a rutted mess. Cal had pulled an old hollow core door out of the construction waste pile, and had made up a sign for out front by the transfer station gate. He had used a half can of salvaged fluorescent pink spray paint. He had planned to write "Welcome Hillary," but the door was not as big as he thought and he ended up with a sign that just read "Welcome Hil."

They had cleaned the hoppers and polished them, but unfortunately, the pelting rain had splashed mud on everything again. Cal had brought over a long yellow rain slicker for Mrs. Clinton. They and the dump were ready for her.

They still had to contend with a steady stream of patrons, townspeople who hoped to time their weekly dump run with the arrival of the ex–first lady-senator-candidate-wanna-be-president. Finally, just about noontime, they spotted the flashing lights on Ed's cruiser. He was followed by three sedans, which had at some point been silver, but now dripped with muddy slurry. Jasper and Cal waited inside the garage to welcome the entourage. Mother had arrived just a few minutes before and was in the office changing out of her rubber galoshes into her best shoes, which were of course, still sensible and appropriate. She was more excited to meet Mrs. Clinton than Jasper was. Mother felt she had an inside perspective, as they both had husbands who often had unpredictable and impractical "notions."

The caravan slid up the drive, nearly running down the Dog Lady as she made the right turn into the yard with her can-laden pick-up truck. When Ed hit his siren lightly to get her attention, she either did not notice, or did not care to give way and continued to creep over to the can packer box. The entire parade came to a halt as the tiny woman, clad in clear plastic poncho and a pair of children's ladybug boots, dragged yet another trash can full of sparkling silver food containers across the yard.

"Aw, Jeezum-crow! Doesn't that dog lady know we got an important to do here today?" Jasper crabbed to Cal.

"That's okay, Jasper, she's leaving. They'll be able to get out soon enough."

Cal and Jasper hesitated. They were prepared, at Mother's suggestion, with an enormous lime green patio umbrella they had found in the Swap Shop. It was seven feet in diameter and they figured that a whole load of people could get under it if need be. Jasper and Cal both ventured out into the mud when the all the vehicle doors opened, except for one. Out poured a hive of black suited young professional types. The women tip-toed and slid in their impractical heels. The men sloshed by them, their trouser legs and shoes caked with mud instantly. They popped open dozens of identical black umbrellas, and at last, the one remaining vehicle door opened and the candidate appeared.

Jasper had grabbed a pile of cardboard out of the corrugated bin and slapped them down into the mud, paving the way to the office door.

"Mrs. Clinton?" he called out, cupping his hands around his mouth to extend the range of his voice. "You jes' step on these cardboards and you can come in here to get going."

Cal waved her over and grabbed her hand as the last piece of old box slid like a boogie board on a good wave and the candidate came close to landing unceremoniously in the mud.

"Well,...um,...Good day, gentlemen," the senator extended her hand into the space in front of them as she righted herself. "What a lovely...and *efficient* facility you have here. Which one of you is Mr. Duckland?" One of her lackeys stood in the rain with his camera flashing at them, while another shoved a huge foam covered microphone in their faces. "I am eager to join with you in a conversation about recycling. I am sure two professionals in the field such as yourselves, with be able to offer us a, um… unique insight on waste management."

Cal grabbed her hand and pumped it exuberantly. He was just a tad jumpy from too much coffee.

"I'm that fella, Miz Clinton! It's great to have you here. Sorry about that slip-slidey there, but you just come on in the station and Jasper'll get you fitted up just right to join in the fun, here!"

The candidate gave her assistant a puzzled glance, but she was yanked unceremoniously, into the office by Cal. Jasper dove at the coffee maker, pouring two cups and presenting one to the candidate. Mother reached out a hand for the other, mistakenly assuming that Jasper had poured it for her. Instead, he raised the mug and sucked in a mouthful.

"Drink up, your Senatorship. This is the good stuff, fresh ground from the store this morning. Tastes damn good, and it'll warm you right up!" He saluted her with a raised cup. She tentatively sipped the brew.

"Mmm, that is,... well,..stimulating! So tell me a bit about your place here, Mr. Dockland… and you are Mr…..? She casually passed her still full mug to Mother.

"Jaspah."

"Mr. Jasper?"

"Just Jaspah. No Mr. needed. Now I don't mean to commandeer you all, but Cal, they're backing up out there. I think we need to get to work!" He slipped the long yellow raincoat over her shoulders and grabbed her arm. "The trash won't wait for no man… or woman!"

In keeping with the spirit of the campaign trail, the former first lady pushed her arms into the sleeves. Mother handed her some black galoshes and quickly helped her slide them on. The two men each firmly grasped a democratic elbow to simultaneously chattering about the benefits and equity of trash, while leading her out to the yard.

Cal and Jasper had moved so smoothly that the entire entourage was caught by surprise. The assistants were still making their way in, negotiating the slippery cardboard, or were still settling wet umbrellas and scoping the building for photo ops. The press van had been lost back at the Four Corners, according to Ed, who had heard this from the cruiser in town. The van had turned left and was headed out on the Crooked Road. He figured they'd realize they were lost when the road peeled off into Gawmers' pig farm.

Jasper and Cal, however, needed no help guiding the candidate from hopper to hopper. Her yellow hooded head bobbed, and she did her best to keep up with them, clomping along in the oversized boots.

"This box is for plastics. We find it is important to keep an eye on this one. Hey, Cal remember that time Seth Mackey threw that dead skunk in there? That cuss! What a stink that put up when we set the crusher on!" Jasper thumped the Senator enthusiastically and continued on. "They don't let any skunks into the White house, eh?"

They headed over to the mulch pile which was steaming with a load of manure fresh from Gawmer's.

"Now here you go, Mrs. Clinton." Cal escorted her to the edge of the pile and grabbed a muddy shovel that had been stuck in the dirt. "Jaspah and I believe that if we do right by our patrons, they in turn will step

127

up and help us out. However, as you know, there are exceptions. Gawmer *never* mixes his manure in, which leaves it to Jaspah and I to take care of every time he comes in. Now, you may not understand the delicate chemical balance required to make a good mulch pile, but if one of those biddies from the garden club - Jaspah - don't you tell Mothuh I said that - gets in here and gets fresh pig poo for their rose gardens, well, I tell ya, all hell is gonna break loose!"

"So, since Old Man Gawmer never mixes in his pig poo, we leave this shovel handy and usually the next fella will give it a turn or two, so Jaspah and I can get our work done. Everyone does their part... Wasn't it you that said it takes a village to raise a child?"

"Well, yes, I did talk about the efforts we as a world and a community need to make... But please, go on, this, is quite enlightening, how would you relate ... um, mixing a manure pile to raising a child? I'm not sure I see the correlation." Mrs. Clinton listened, patiently, yet a bit bemused.

"Well, it's as plain as that pile of steaming poop. It takes a village to mix the compost. We're a community. Me and Jaspah, we can't do it all on our own. Recycling and reusing is about people helping each other out." Cal smiled. "Here, take the shovel. Give it a try, your honor."

With that, he jammed the handle into her hand and gave her a polite poke toward the pile. She looked back for her aides- or anyone- but realized no one was going to save her from this campaign task. She lifted an oversized boot and pushed the shovel into the runny, future fertilizer and gave it a valiant flip. She quickly handed the shovel off to Cal and diplomatically redirected them by asking about their obvious efforts to separate a variety of items.

"Oh yeah, at first it was hard and we got a little carried away. We had about two dozen bins out here and were sorting everything by number or type – you know like foil cake pans, foil wrapping, baggies, regular cans, beer cans, then you know those weird potato chip cans that really aren't cans?" Jasper had jumped on this topic as he was the champion of all sorters. He could sort for hours, if it meant he wasn't doing something that was more like work. "You must've had them Pringles. You must get those for Bill, eh? He seems to like his snacks! But they have foil sides and a metal bottom and plastic on top. How the heck are we supposed to find a place for them? So," he said with a sigh, "I made another barrel for them, wash them out and we give 'em over to the preschool for projects. You should see that woman over there when I drive up, the look on her face it like she never saw so many of those things."

"But that's what we do here. We find places where people need what we have. You should do that too. You maybe could find a place where they have a ton of kids and don't have any sand…So you go to the foreigners and tell them. Then they have a place to sell their sand and they got a little trade goin'. They got business and they don't have time to fight any more. See how it works?" Jasper and Cal nodded in agreement.

"That is a very interesting idea, gentlemen." The senator wiped a trickle of rain from her face with the corduroy cuff on the slicker. Unfortunately, some of Gawmer's pig stuff was still on the coat and unbeknownst to the candidate her cheek now bore a distinctive dark brown streak. "Exchange of products and encouraging free trade between countries is a huge piece of our platform."

"Aw, I don't think those kids need a platform. The sand will be good enough probably." Jasper concluded.

At this point, the man with the camera and microphone had caught up with the tour, and Cal tugged the Senator over to the main trash hopper to meet some of the locals. He had noticed that they were all unloading their vehicles with unusual slowness. There was now a line of cars backed out to the front gate. The senator was instinctively gracious, and she also knew how to take advantage of an unusual photo op. She shook hands and posed in front of trash filled vehicles. She even helped George Edwards heave his bags into the hopper. George was eighty-seven years old and as thin and bent as paper clip. He was grinning ear to ear when they heaved his last bag over the fence together and everyone cheered.

Finally, Cal and Jasper carefully guide her away from the Dog Lady's truck. The strange little woman had been methodically lobbing single shiny cans into a bin. When they ducked past her, there was a distinctive 'ting' of cans hitting the small area of pavement behind them, closer each time. When they were out of range they glanced back. The tiny woman stood by her vehicle glaring at Mrs. Clinton.

"Ahh, Miz Clinton, it might be bettah if we all head back to the cover of the office just now." Cal declared. "Besides, while we're finishing our tour here, I just want to make sure that you got a good look at a place where everyone is equal! Jaspah and I are proud to be able to serve the residents." Cal extended his arms in a blessing of the entire facility. "You gotta understand what trash means to this world. I mean everyone makes it. You, your husband, heck, even the Pope himself makes trash...and you can't say that about many things with him! So you gonna take some of this on in your camp-pining?" He waved his hand, gesturing over the expanse of the facility.

"Camp-pining?" Hillary Clinton peered out from under the brim of the over sized hood she wore. Rain water dripped down her face, and had ruined what had

131

previously been a pristine make-up job. Her legs above Mother's boots were spattered with mud. The edge of her fine red wool skirt was soaked and stained with manure. Impatience had finally edged into her voice. "I don't camp. What in the world are you talking about?"

"*Camp-pining* – going out to get the vote, like you're doin' here. The Village – you said yourself- it does take a village! We see it here everyday. It takes the whole town to fill this place. It takes the Dog Lady, Gawmer, picky Joe Garner, and George Edwards to fill this place. Without them we wouldn't be here. Heck-you wouldn't be here either!" Cal spun around satisfied that anyone could see the plain truth of his philosophy.

Incredulous, the woman gazed at him.

"*What...?*" She turned to Jasper as a source of reason. She was hopeful that he could at the very least interpret. "*What* is he talking about?"

Jasper leaned in close, whispering into her hooded ear.

"Damned if I know what he's yappin' about, lady. If I was you, I'd jest smile. Ask him if he thinks there's anymore coffee left. It always works for me when he gets blabbing like this!"

The woman, who hoped to take on the nation and the world, took Jasper's advice, and in a moment they were headed back to the shop. Cal continued to espouse that the communion of people and trash was the answer to all the world's problems. Jasper and Mrs. Clinton mostly ignored him. The candidate peeled back the yellow hood, signaling anxiously to the driver of her car to come around.

Unfortunately, the driver, and the balance of her staff, had been caught up in the spirit of the day and were eagerly combing through the Swap Shop for treasures of their own.

Mother had put the coffee on and had served up slices of nut bread on the bamboo bar. The light of the naked goddess lamp twinkled warmly inside the small room, welcoming the boys and their guest back. She knew that even a seasoned politician and former first lady, would need a debriefing after spending any time with Cal and Jasper. With one arm, Mother swung the door open welcoming the other woman into the office. With the other arm, Mother barred Jasper and Cal from following.

"Dears, why don't you go down and see what those nice boys have found in the Swap Shop will you? I heard one say he found some sort of fancy radio and all it needs is a couple of new knobs!" Jasper swung around and slid down the path to the barn. Cal started running. The last the two women saw were the pair of mud covered men falling over each other to get to the barn first.

Mother turned to the former first lady, handed her a clean towel, and began to help her out of the dripping rain coat.

"So tell me Mrs. Clinton, would you like a hand taking off those boots? I bet you have learned a few things today, haven't you, dear?"

www.ingramcontent.com/pod-product-compliance
Lightning Source LLC
Chambersburg PA
CBHW060230180626
46813CB00007B/3024